Attack at Pearl Harbor

Liberty Letters®

Attack at Pearl Harbor

Previously published as *The Personal Correspondence of Catherine Clark and Meredith Lyons*

Nancy LeSourd

ZONDERVAN.com/
AUTHORTRACKER
follow your favorite authors

Attack at Pearl Harbor
Previously published as *The Personal Correspondence of Catherine Clark and Meredith Lyons*
Copyright © 2003, 2008 by Nancy Oliver LeSourd

Requests for information should be addressed to:
Zonderkidz, Grand Rapids, Michigan 49530

Library of Congress Cataloging-in-Publication Data

LeSourd, Nancy.-
    Attack at Pearl Harbor / by Nancy LeSourd.
       p. cm. -- (Liberty letters).
    Previously published in slightly altered form under title: The personal correspondence of
Catherine Clark and Meredith Lyons. 2004.
    Summary: Letters between two young girls, one in Washington, D.C., and eager to become
a newspaper reporter, the other in Pearl Harbor, Hawaii, determined to take flying lessons,
chronicle not only events in the year leading up to the 1941 attack on Pearl Harbor, but also the
pain of having their fathers in the war. Includes epilogue with facts and photographs.
      ISBN 978-0-310-71389-0 (softcover)
      1. World War, 1939-1945--Juvenile fiction. [1. World War, 1939-1945--Fiction. 2. Reporters and
reporting--Fiction. 3. Airplanes--Piloting--Fiction. 4. Christian life--Fiction. 5. Letters--Fiction.] I.
LeSourd, Nancy. Personal correspondence of Catherine Clark and Meredith Lyons. II. Title.
    PZ7.L56268At 2008
    [Fic]--dc22

          2008014493

Editor: Barbara Scott
Art direction & cover design: Merit Alderink
Interior design: Carlos Eluterio Estrada
Cover illustrator: Guy Porfirio

Printed in the United States of America

In Honor of Jim Downing
Gunners Mate, USS West Virginia
Pearl Harbor Veteran
Twenty-Four Years in the U.S. Navy
Thirty Years on Staff with the Navigators
Ephesians 3:20

In Memory of Len LeSourd
Pilot, U.S. Army Air Corps, 43-G
Author, Sky-Bent
Editor, Author, Publisher, Father-in-Law, and Friend
Proverbs 3:5 and 6

Somewhere Over the Pacific Ocean

OCTOBER 25, 1940

Dear Catherine,

Mother always says my big mouth gets me into trouble. But today it got me into the cockpit of a Clipper Ship!

Granddaddy insisted we take the Pan Am Clipper for the last part of our trip from San Francisco to Pearl Harbor. When Mother said it was too expensive, he said we'll use military vehicles for the rest of our lives. He wanted us to have this once-in-a-lifetime experience.

But that's just it. If this is the only time I'm on a flying airship, I've got to truly experience it. That's where an eight-year-old brother who can't sit still comes in handy. I told Mother I'd watch Gordon while he went to explore. Mother leaned back, closed her eyes, and murmured, "Uh huh," which I took to mean yes.

Gordo has no clue how lucky we are to fly on a Clipper Ship. This flying ship can land on water, has places for us to sleep, and makes it possible to cross oceans in days instead of weeks. Gordo wanted to find out if a celebrity was in the deluxe cabin, but I was tired of the passenger deck. We'd already spent a lot of time here. I tugged at my dress, which had wrinkled dreadfully. I'd have to change for dinner, for sure. We've eaten all our meals in the elegant dining room with its starched white tablecloths, gleaming china and crystal, and sterling silverware. Mother insisted we dress to match. I think it's stupid to wear my white gloves to dinner, just to take them off, and try not to get any food on them.

As we walked along the passenger deck, we kept bumping into stewards wanting to fulfill my every need. "Juice, Miss Lyons?" "Another blanket, Miss Lyons?" "Care for tea, Miss Lyons?" Very annoying. What I wanted to see was the cockpit, but I didn't dare ask the steward for that. After poking around the deluxe cabin and finding no sign of a Hollywood star, Gordo was finally willing to go upstairs to the crew deck.

A small sign said "Personnel Only," but I pretended I didn't see it. While the stewards were busy, we crept up the staircase. Gordo was drawn to chocolate chip cookie smells coming from the kitchen (they call it a galley), but I pulled him on down the hall. We inched past a room where a crew member sorted mail into three different mailbags Gordo's size. The door next to the mail room flung open. We hid in its shadow as a uniformed man with papers folded under his arm marched down the hall. The sign on the door said "Navigation."

"He's headed to the cockpit," I whispered. "Let's follow him."

"Are you crazy?" Gordo said. "They're gonna kick us out of here."

"Thousands of feet above the Pacific Ocean? I don't think so. But if you're scared, go back downstairs to Mother."

Gordo shook his head, but stayed behind me as I walked toward the cockpit. We slipped by the mail room and the kitchen. The cook sang at the top of his lungs while he banged pots and pans. Gordo started giggling. I elbowed him hard, for we were right outside the cockpit door. I heard voices inside that door. "What ya gonna do now?" whispered Gordo.

The door handle turned, and I held my breath. A uniformed man stepped out of the cockpit. "Well, well, what do we have here?"

Gordo shrank back behind me. I put out my gloved hand. "Hello, sir, I'm Meredith Lyons."

"Pleased to meet you, Miss Lyons, and you too, young Master Lyons, I assume?" Gordo nodded. "Hmm ... A bit off course, are you? The stairs to the passenger deck are right over there."

Gordo started toward the stairs, and I yanked him back. "Sir, I wondered if we could see the cockpit? We've never been on an airship before."

"Not really allowed, young lady, but I'll check with the captain." He disappeared back into the cockpit. A few minutes later, he cracked the door and said, "Sorry, but you'll have to return to the passenger deck."

I stepped forward and put my foot right inside the door so that the officer couldn't shut it. He looked annoyed, but I was

determined to get inside. "Sir, you see, my whole life I've wanted to see inside a cockpit. I keep a scrapbook of all these articles about flying and planes and Amelia Earhart and everything. Sir, did you know, not too long ago, she took a photograph of a Clipper flying to California while she was flying her plane to Honolulu? Isn't that something! This might even be the exact same plane Amelia Earhart took a picture of! Everyone's been so nice down below, but it's what you important men do up here that really interests me. Please, sir. Won't you ask one more time?"

Gordo looked like he was going to die and begged me to leave before the man came back. I told him, "No way."

It seemed like an hour, but finally the officer opened the door, and said, "After you, Miss Lyons." I pushed by Gordo to get inside before the officer changed his mind.

The captain checked the dials and instruments in front of him. The other pilot scribbled something in a large brown logbook. Numbers, I think. The navigator scooted over and let Gordo sit next to him. The copilot stood up, and pointing to his seat, said, "Miss Lyons?"

As I slipped into the seat, I stared at the vast expanse of sky before me. The stars lit up the inky darkness surrounding the plane. After a few minutes, the copilot asked me what I thought. I blinked hard. The stars were still there. Without taking my eyes off the window, I whispered, "Thank you."

Back downstairs in our seats, Gordo went on and on about what he'd seen in the cockpit. Mother was furious at me. "Young lady, your father and I try to teach you what's right and proper, but you constantly amaze me. How dare you bother those pilots while they're doing their job? You know better. And to get Gordon caught up in your scheme too. Won't you ever learn?" I stared out the window and tried to block it all out. This wasn't a good time to bring up my wanting to learn to fly again. I heard Mother's voice in my head. "Absolutely not. It's simply not an option." We'd been through this a million times before over the last few years.

No, not even today on my birthday would this be a good topic of conversation.

I apologized to Mother for bothering the pilots, being a bad example for Gordo, embarrassing her, and not conducting myself as the daughter of a Naval officer. I said all the right things, but inside I was glad I'd done it. I'll never forget turning sixteen. Somehow, some way, before I turn seventeen, I'll find a way to fly.

Maybe this new assignment to Pearl Harbor will be the start of something new. After all, they call Hawaii "paradise," and what would be more heavenly than taking off into the skies, circling the clouds, and landing again—all by myself.

Your high-flying friend,

Mettie

Norfolk, Virginia

NOVEMBER 1, 1940

Dear Merrie,

I've missed you! Norfolk's not the same without you. Guess what? Dad got transfer orders to the Naval Air Station at Kaneohe. We're coming to Hawaii too!

Mom makes lists and posts them everywhere—the bathroom mirror, the refrigerator, the car dashboard. Mom and Dad talk late at night. There's much to do to get Dad ready to go, and with Hank and all, it's a challenge.

When I visited Hank today, Nurse Reynolds told me the Naval Hospital's right on the water. I can picture my brother with a bed next to a large window so he can see the palm trees and feel the warm breezes. It might make up for these horrid six months in the iron lung.

Standing next to Hank's head and talking to him, I try to block out the sounds of the iron prison he's been in for these last six months. Every day I've visited him, I've hated that machine, even though it helps him breathe as it pushes and pulls the air in his chest.

I remember listening to the radio with Hank a few months ago, when Sea Biscuit set that new track record. Hank shouted as loud as he could when the machine would let him speak. Whoosh-whooo. "Go, Biscuit!" Whoosh-whoo. "You can—" Whoosh-whoo "—do it, boy." The announcer said this patched-up crippled horse roared to the finish line in the last stretch of the race. I could see in Hank's eyes that he wants to be just like Biscuit—a down-and-out, "patched-up cripple" who astonishes people with what he can do. Hank's determined to walk again, but his determination breaks my heart. I feel so guilty keeping the truth from him, but I don't have the nerve to tell him what the doctors told us.

You remember what a great baseball player Hank was before he got polio—especially last year on his seventh-grade team? Boy, could he hit! I'll never forget the crack of the bat as it connected with the ball every time. But now, the only sports he can play are in his head. When Hank listens to games on the radio, he forgets he can't move his legs and pretends he's his old self again. That's just it, though, it's all pretend.

Mom wants me to spend more time with my friends, but I know how much Hank looks forward to my visits. I feel so guilty if I don't come by. When I go to the movies with my friends, I feel like I shouldn't enjoy myself. After all, what fun does Hank have in that iron prison? I tell myself I go to the movies to see the newsreels, to write articles for the school paper. It's like I can't allow myself to just enjoy the movie. Not when Hank's been through so much. I know I'm protective of Hank, but golly, he can't even breathe on his own. Sometimes I hate all this. I wish things were back the way they were—before Hank got sick.

Your friend,

Catherine

Pearl Harbor, Hawaii

NOVEMBER 13, 1940

Dear Catherine,

I can't wait until you get here! I told Mother and Dad right away. Gordo's announced to one and all that his best friend, Hank, is coming. Hank's such a good sport to put up with this hero worship.

I can walk to the tennis courts right next to the hospital. I've been playing almost every day, but I miss my favorite doubles partner. Hurry up and get here! I need your help to discourage all these grown-ups who think I'm going to grow up to be just like Mother.

You know the drill the first weeks at a new base. Lots of official visits, shaking hands, and being polite. Last week, when the officers and their wives visited us, I must have heard ten times, "What a lovely girl. Is she going to train to be a nurse?"

I cringed as I heard Mother's stock answer, "Our Meredith could do worse than join us in the medical field or in the Navy."

I faked smiles and shook hands with beautiful officers' wives and pretended to listen. I did okay until this one woman, Mrs. Eagleton. She kept pestering me about my nursing plans and asked thousands of questions. She insisted I come to her house Tuesday night to roll bandages for the war effort in England. Her daughter, Gwendolyn, who's my age, will be there. Mother answered for me and said I'd come. I hate it when she does that.

No, I don't want to be a nurse. And I don't want to be in the Navy. Unless, of course, they'll let me be a pilot. But no women can do that now. And roll bandages? That's just more of the same nursing junk Mother wants me to learn.

Come Tuesday, Mother dropped me off at Mrs. Eagleton's home with strips of cotton cloth and her best surgical scissors. Mrs. Eagleton introduced me to everyone as "the daughter of Captain

William J. Lyons, that new surgeon at the hospital, and the lovely Navy nurse, Marilyn Lyons." The women all ooohed and aahhhed. Here it comes, I thought.

"Meredith's going to study to be a nurse too." Inwardly I groaned, but I replied, "Nice to meet you," and took a seat at the dining room table at the farthest end from Mrs. Eagleton, next to the only other girl my age. I plopped my basket of cloth strips on the table.

"I wanted to be a nurse too," Mrs. Eagleton's daughter, Gwendolyn, said. "One day I volunteered at the hospital, but the smells just didn't agree with me."

"It's not for everyone," I replied. Gwendolyn's beautiful. She has long curly red hair and a few perfect freckles across her perfect nose. I stared at her sitting there in her freshly ironed dress. She looked every bit an officer's daughter. Not at all like me. Give me a ponytail and a tennis outfit any day. As Gwendolyn rolled her bandages, I stared at her long slender fingers and painted nails. I curled my fingers to hide the two broken nails from my tennis game.

Mrs. Eagleton jingled a small handbell she kept by her place. An Asian woman, head down, handed fruit punch drinks to everyone. She backed out of the room with her empty tray still held high and gave little nods as she disappeared into the kitchen. Mrs. Eagleton asked, "Has your mother found a maid yet, Meredith? She simply cannot make it here without good help. Not with two children and her duties, you know."

I didn't know. We'd gotten along fine so far, it seemed to me.

"The Jap girls are the best. Why, I've never had a bit of trouble with mine. I check my jewelry after every time she's here. So far, she hasn't taken a thing." Can you believe that pompous old bat said that? Then she said, "I'll get your mother a reference right away. You can't be too careful these days—with the war coming and all."

"Why, I've never had a bit of trouble with mine." So are they some kind of possession? I think not. They're people! They've got names! "You can't be too careful these days." Yeah, like right now. I think I need to be careful who I associate with. Geez, Louise, these

people are opinionated! I sure hope Mother doesn't get a maid. If she does, she'd better not call her "her girl."

Gwendolyn made the night bearable and filled me in on the dances, the boys, and the teachers at Roosevelt High. I started school there the next day. Her boyfriend is a football star. Figures. At the end of the evening, I had stacks of rolled bandages and was exhausted from being nice to Mrs. Eagleton. You'll have to thank me later for going through all this first! Hurry and get here. I need someone normal to talk to.

Your friend,

Merrie

Pearl Harbor, Hawaii

November 17, 1940

Dear Catherine,

School's not so bad here. Lots of Navy kids. Gwendolyn showed me around Roosevelt High the first week. I've never met so many football players. Gwendolyn introduced me to her boyfriend's friends on the team, but they're not my type. I spotted someone who could be though! His name's Drew Masterson. He's in two of my classes, and his father's a pilot with the Army Air Corps. One minor problem: he doesn't know I exist.

Today I went to Waikiki Beach to play volleyball with some kids from school. Gwendolyn watched us play. She didn't want to break a nail. There was another volleyball game going on nearby. When I asked her where those other kids went to school, she said, "Tokyo High."

"What?"

"McKinley High. They've got their school, and we've got ours."

The Japanese thing again. They looked like nice kids to me. I walked over to one of the girls taking a break from her game. "Great serve," I said.

"Thanks!"

"I'm Merrie Lyons. Just moved here from Virginia."

"I'm Janet. Janet Tanaka. Navy or Army?"

"Does it show?"

Janet laughed. "Oahu is overrun with you military kids. Mostly Navy."

"You got it. Navy it is. My parents are at the Naval Hospital. Dad's a doctor; Mother's a nurse."

"Brothers and sisters?" Janet asked.

"One brother. Eight. A real pain."

"Two brothers. Ten and eleven. Definitely a pain."

We talked for half an hour. She's a junior at McKinley High.

Her real name is Miyoko, but she likes her American name, Janet. Her father won't call her anything but Miyoko. He teaches at the Japanese Language School. Miyoko said her parents' generation is worried the kids born in Hawaii will forget all about the ways of Japan and not want to speak Japanese anymore.

"I speak Japanese at home, go by Miyoko, and attend my father's Language School. But as soon as I'm out the door, I'm Janet. Speaking English. Just like this."

Miyoko means "beautiful," and it's a beautiful name. I wish she'd call herself that. But she made it clear, she's "Janet." My friends waved for me to come on. As I went to join them, I realized something. Not once did Miyoko ask me if I was going to be a nurse.

Your friend,

Merrie

Pearl Harbor, Hawaii

November 24, 1940

Dear Catherine,

Get this. There's going to be an aviation course at school next semester! No actual flying, but the instructor's a pilot, and the course covers everything you need to know from the ground. I was the third person to sign up. I checked the sign-up sheet again today. There're twenty-four kids signed up. So far I'm the only girl. I can't wait!

Dad and Mother take us to the Royal Hawaiian Hotel every Saturday afternoon for the tea dances. This week, I saw that boy I like, Drew. He danced the entire time, but not with me. Am I invisible or something? But wow, can he jitterbug!

Gwendolyn was there with her boyfriend, Joe. She made sure all his friends asked me to dance, but I would have traded them all for one dance with Drew. The bands are terrific. Local Hawaiian music mixed right in with Glen Miller and Tommy Dorsey. (Don't you just love "Blueberry Hill"?) The kids here are great dancers. The jitterbug's a slight favorite over the lindy. It's a swell way to meet kids. I'll take you with me the first Saturday you're here.

Gordo wants you to tell Hank "Captain Midnight" is on the radio here too. Here's a note for Hank in secret code. We had to drink gallons of Ovaltine before Gordo collected enough seals to send in for Captain Midnight's Code-O-Graph. Trouble is, Hank has to be able to use his hands, or he won't know what it says. I'll try to find out from Gordo. Right now, he pretends I'm the evil enemy agent and if I get the secret code, all of America will die. Gordo, of course, will save the world since he's the ace aviator, valiant member of Captain Midnight's Secret Squadron (along with every other kid in America!).

I like our Bible class teacher, Jim Downing. He's a gunners mate on the battleship USS *West Virginia* and leads a Bible study on his ship. He's part of a Navigators Bible study in Honolulu too. I told him our fathers were both in a Navigators Bible study back in Norfolk. All the kids like him a lot.

You'll love it here. I'll remind you how to have guilt-free fun again! And you'll be here to keep me out of trouble!

Your friend,

Merrie

Norfolk, Virginia

DECEMBER 2, 1940

Dear Merrie,

I've got the most horrible news. I still can't believe it. Daddy leaves in ten days for Pearl Harbor. Alone! All those late-night discussions Mom and Dad had? Well, they were making decisions all right, but not about what to pack. We're not going with Daddy to Pearl Harbor. And it gets worse. They're sending Hank away to Georgia!

I begged them to change their minds. Daddy says the doctors want to wean Hank off the iron lung, and then Hank can get rehabilitation for his legs. The doctors say the best place for that is Warm Springs Foundation in Georgia.

I do want Hank to get better. You know I do. But he needs us too. I asked Mom if we could move to Warm Springs. Mom said it's not possible. When I asked why not, she and Dad looked funny but didn't say anything. I told them if Hank can't come to Hawaii, then I want Mom and me to go to Georgia. Who else will bring him the sports pages and read to him? Who else will wipe away his tears after the nurses tighten his braces? Who else will listen to those silly sports games with him? I have to be near him. He needs me.

Your friend,

Catherine

Pearl Harbor, Hawaii

December 4, 1940

Dear Catherine,

Someone scratched my name off the aviation class sign-up sheet. I figured it was some spiteful boy who hadn't signed up in time and wanted to make sure he got in the class. I marched myself down to the school office to complain. You know what I found out? No girls can take the aviation course! I can't believe it.

Mrs. Hatchett, the school secretary, sniffed and said, "Besides, young lady, you're the only girl who signed up. That ought to tell you something." She shoved another sign-up sheet across the counter in front of me. "Perhaps you'd rather take the Nutrition and Health elective?"

Perhaps I'd rather not! So what if I'm the only girl that wants to take the aviation course? I may be the only girl with enough guts to fly. Being a girl shouldn't matter. Just five years ago, Amelia Earhart flew out of Honolulu to be the first person—man or woman, thank you—to cross the Atlantic Ocean *by herself.* I bet if Amelia Earhart were still alive, she'd have a thing or two to say about this rule.

"Who do I need to see to get into the class?"

"Young lady. A rule is a rule. No girls."

"Gee, that's really too bad. Who is going to teach this class anyway?"

"Mr. Lindstrom. Works for Andrews Flying Service. Fine aviator."

I signed up for the nutrition class, smiled sweetly at the secretary, then headed for the nearest phone book. Andrews Flying Service. John Rodgers Airport. I called Mother and told her I'd be home late. School business to take care of. The whole way to the airfield on the bus, I rehearsed my speech. "Mr. Lindstrom, I have to take this course. I've wanted to fly since I was eleven. I've been clipping articles on women aviatrixes for years. You should see my scrapbook. Amy Johnson. Amelia Earhart. Jackie Cochran. All great women pilots. They've broken all kinds of records. There's no reason girls should be excluded from this course. I know I'm the only one who signed up, but we can start a trend."

The bus squealed as it stopped in front of the hangar. When I stepped out, the musky smell of oil fumes mixed with the fresh scent of grass. Someone started the propeller on a trainer plane. The *whish whish whish whish* sounded like the beat of a bird's wings in flight. I took a deep breath and closed my eyes. Oh, how I wanted to be in the sky. But first things first. I walked to the largest hangar, found some men who looked like pilots, and asked for the office of Andrews Flying Service. They pointed to a desk covered with coffee cups set up in a dreary corner. On the wall next to the desk was a big calendar with names and times scribbled all over it. I was ready to give my speech, but there was no one there to give it to.

A girl in coveralls walked over and said, "Can I help you?"

"I'm looking for Mr. Lindstrom, the flight instructor."

"He's up in the air right now. Anything I can do for you?" I studied her. She was about nineteen or twenty years old, with gorgeous hair. She looked out of place in the coveralls. She stuck out a hand smeared with grease. I shook it anyway. "Name's Betty Guild," she said. "I work for Mr. Andrews."

"Oh, do you book the flights? I saw the calendar."

"Sure. We're always busy here. Tourists love to go flight-seeing."

"I've heard about that. Island hopping, right? I'd love to go up in a plane. Must be expensive, though."

"Well, it does pay the rent. Mr. Lindstrom will be landing at the runway over there if you want to wait for him."

I thanked her, and as I walked down to the gravel runway at the other end of the hangars, I rehearsed my speech again. About twenty minutes later, Mr. Lindstrom landed the bright yellow Piper Cub on the gravel strip and taxied to the end of the runway where I was waiting.

I started to greet him, when I heard Miss Guild behind me. "Got enough gas for one more run, Jerry?" He nodded. They did a quick check of the plane. Jerry wiped something off the celluloid windshield and then gave Betty a thumbs-up sign. She tossed him her clipboard, climbed into the open cockpit, adjusted her goggles, and gave him a nod. He pulled on the propeller to start it spinning. She turned the plane and picked up speed as she taxied down the runway. So the woman in the coveralls was a pilot!

I'll never forget the rush of the wind blowing my hair as I shaded my eyes from the sun. The sight of that little plane lifting gently into the air, and flown by a girl pilot not much older than me, made me even more determined.

I turned to find Mr. Lindstrom already halfway back to the hangar. I raced after him. When I caught up to him, I was out of breath. The words tumbled out of my mouth, all mixed up with the excitement of what I had just seen. He stood there, arms folded and eyebrows raised, like he was trying not to laugh at me. I didn't care. I just had to get a place in that class.

"And so, Mr. Lindstrom, I need you to tell my school that it's okay for me to be in your class."

Now he did laugh. "Well, young lady, that was some speech. Your name?"

"Meredith Lyons. I'm sixteen."

"You see that pilot there ..." He motioned to Miss Guild, now high in the sky. "She soloed by the time she was fifteen. You're behind!"

"Then I need to catch up, starting with being in your class. Please, sir, can you go to bat for me?"

"Well, I can't promise anything, but I'll ask. You know schools though. Full of rules."

"Don't I know it! Rules that make no sense whatsoever."

"Well, now, I'm not so sure about that, young lady. You see, there's a war on, and those boys are gonna be needed soon. For every gal that takes up a spot, that's one less future flying ace ready to take on those Germans."

"Yes, sir, but how do we know they won't need women pilots in this war too?"

Well, he laughed so hard, I could barely make out what he said. "Okay, little lady, I'll get back to you with an answer."

When Mom asked where I'd been, I told her I was trying to get into a tough class. When she asked what it was, I braced myself and told her aviation. She hit the ceiling. Once I explained it was only a ground course, no flying, she calmed down a little. I still got a big lecture about not wasting my courses. She said to be careful about what I pick to study and make sure it can help me in the future. That's exactly what I did! But not in her opinion. When she found out my other choice was the nutrition class, she said that's much more practical for nursing school. I'm done sharing my dreams with her. She just doesn't get it.

Tonight I wrote the name Betty Guild on my brochure from Andrews Flying Service I picked up today. By the picture of the Piper Cub, I wrote my name, then hid it in my scrapbook under my bed. I hope Mr. Lindstrom took me seriously. I'll just die if I can't take that class.

Your friend,

Merrie

Pearl Harbor, Hawaii

DECEMBER 7, 1940

Dear Catherine,

Gwendolyn and I went to the Roosevelt football game and sat with the other football players' girlfriends. Talk about boring! They giggled, talked about fashions, and weren't even watching the game. I finally excused myself and sat with my friends, Frank and Helen. I saw Drew in the stands during the second half of the game. I'd sure like to get to know him better.

A bunch of kids went to the Coconut Shack after the game. Drew stopped by our table to speak to Frank. I pretended like I wasn't interested in him, but my face got all hot. He never said a word to me. He's rough on my ego! Frank asked him how his flight lesson went that morning. As Drew talked, I acted like I wasn't listening, but I caught everything he said.

Helen elbowed me and asked me if I thought he was handsome. I shushed her. Later, Helen said Drew has only one thing on his mind these days, and that's flying. I can't say I blame him. I wonder who his flight instructor is. Probably not Miss Guild.

One weird thing happened. Drew and Frank were talking about the latest Captain Midnight episode! Apparently, Captain Midnight recovered microfilm from the world mastermind criminal, the Barracuda. And what's on the film? A diagram of Pearl Harbor. Drew and Frank argued about its meaning. Frank thinks the Barracuda was hired to smuggle saboteurs and equipment to the Hawaiian Islands to be ready in case the war gets worse. Drew thinks it's more devious than that, that it's part of a plan for attack, and the Barracuda might sell the diagram to the highest bidder.

Drew must have seen my face because suddenly he looked very sheepish. "My father listens to Captain Midnight," he said. Oh yeah,

like that explains it. I was tempted to ask if he had his very own Code-O-Graph, but I bit my tongue. Writing this now, I can't help but laugh. Imagine Drew up in the air during his lesson, pretending he's Captain Midnight, super fighting ace. Saving the world.

Your friend,

Merrie

Norfolk, Virginia

DECEMBER 8, 1940

Dear Merrie,

I went to the hospital today after church to listen to the Redskins championship game on the radio with Hank. It was horrible. The nurse finished the friction massage of his legs — that alone hurts him a lot — then she put Hank's braces back on. When she tightened them, he cried out in such awful pain. I reached out and touched his face — the only part of him I can see in that horrid iron lung. He seemed embarrassed and wouldn't look at me. How will he survive when he's alone in Georgia? He's going to need me there.

We listened to the most miserable football game. The Redskins lost 73 to 0. The radio announcer shouted "blistering defeat" and "utter annihilation." Hank snapped at me and told me to go home. He said he wanted to be alone. If he only knew how alone he's about to be, he wouldn't push me away. We have so little time left.

Daddy's coming tonight to tell Hank about Georgia. I'm sure he'll beg Daddy to let us go with him. It's the only thing that makes sense. Mom can get a job in Georgia. I can go to school there. We can't leave Hank alone. My brother needs me.

Your friend,

Catherine

Norfolk, Virginia

DECEMBER 12, 1940

Dear Merrie,

Daddy shipped out today. You'll see him soon. I won't. Daddy and Mom waited until last night to tell me one more piece of news about our family. Just when I didn't think it could get any worse. Daddy's moving to Hawaii. Hank's moving to Georgia. Now Mom and I are moving to Washington, D.C.! I can't stand this. I feel like my whole world is crashing down. Life as I knew it is over!

Mom's going to work in the White House secretarial pool for Mrs. Roosevelt to help pay for Hank's rehabilitation. The job there pays more than any she could get in Norfolk or Warm Springs. But I don't want to move. It's bad enough I'm losing my brother. Do I have to lose my school and my friends too just when I became a reporter for the school newspaper? Why can't it be like it was before? Before the polio. Oh, why can't our family stay together?

Mom's job starts after the first of the year. There's hardly any time to say good-bye to our friends. We'll spend Christmas in Warm Springs to help Hank settle in, then take the train straight to Washington. Just like that, I'll start at a new school. Alone, without my father. Alone, without my brother. Alone, without my best friend.

This is the saddest Christmas ever.

Your friend,

Catherine

Pearl Harbor, Hawaii

Dear Catherine,

I can't believe you're not moving here! You must be so upset. I am too! And Hank! What'll he do without you? You know exactly what to do to make him laugh and give him hope. I've watched you with him. He depends on you.

I've depended on you too. I thought about you when I looked through my scrapbook last night. So many of these articles about girl pilots are the ones you clipped for me. Sometimes you wrote something in the margin. "This will be you one day." "Invite me to your solo flight." "Merrie Lyons, future aviatrix." I thought of all the times you kept me from making a big mess out of something. My passion plus your cool determination. We made a great team. I need you next door again!

This was not a good week for news. Once again, Mrs. Hatchett called me to the school office. "I understand you did some lobbying for admission to the aviation course. Rather unorthodox. We have rules for a reason." She smoothed her flyaway hair and shuffled some papers on the counter. Then she lowered her glasses to the tip of her nose to peer over them at me. "Mr. Lindstrom has prevailed upon us to let you take the course. Before you get too excited, young lady, there's a condition. You must maintain a B average in math this semester. I checked with your math teacher. She said you have a C- average right now, and only the final exam is left." She smirked and turned away.

Pull a C- up to a B with only one exam? It's three days away! That's next to impossible, but I'm going to study like crazy.

Your friend,

Merrie

On the Train to Warm Springs

DECEMBER 20, 1940

Dear Merrie,

We're only hours away now. We changed trains in Atlanta to take this one to Warm Springs. Hank's done fairly well on the trip.

Over the last few weeks, the staff at the hospital weaned Hank off the iron lung. I was scared he'd have trouble breathing on his own, but he's been okay. He was eager to be free of his iron prison, so much so that he doesn't mind his wheelchair. It looks like another metal prison to me.

Instead of being disappointed about the move to Georgia, Hank's excited. He told me he's going to learn to walk again and then play baseball. "Maybe for the Yankees. Lou Gehrig better watch out!"

I couldn't believe it. I wanted to scream, "Stop it. You're never going to walk again, and you have to accept it. Warm Springs is just another hospital. It's no baseball stadium, and you're no Yankee baseball star." I was shocked at my feelings, and I know it's wrong, but I'm so angry. This polio has ruined our family, and I'm sick of it. It took Hank's dreams away from him, and now because of it, it's taking my dreams away from me. It makes it worse to have to pretend this is a great thing, but that's what Mom wants me to do—for Hank's sake. But that's all we've been doing for a year now. Every decision we make is for Hank's sake. All because of this hateful disease. Now, I'm spending Christmas dropping off my brother in some strange state and thinking about my father halfway across the world—all because of polio.

Your friend,

Catherine

Pearl Harbor, Hawaii

December 21, 1940

Dear Catherine,

I have no idea how I did on the math final. Dad quizzed me every night and I asked for extra help from the teacher. But is it enough?

Gwendolyn, Helen, and I went Christmas shopping. We stayed for dinner so we could see the lights. The Christmas trees arrived from the mainland a few days ago. Dad's picking one up for us today. My favorite present is what I got for Gordo — a harmonica! I saw his eyes light up when one of the sailors played his harmonica at our house last month (when Mother had some of the men from the *West Virginia* over for Sunday dinner). I got Mother a necklace made out of puka shells. I hope she'll let me borrow it. Dad's always hard to shop for, but not this year. I got him a Hawaiian shirt. Can't you picture him dressed in the flowered shirt, wearing a lei, playing his ukulele, and singing at the top of his lungs?

I wish I could give Gordo his present early. He's been moping around for days since he heard Hank isn't coming. He wants to know if he can go to Georgia to visit Hank. Can you imagine what that would cost? Mother told him it might be possible. Yeah, about as possible as Captain Midnight setting down his plane at John Rodgers airfield.

We ran into Miyoko downtown. I mean Janet. I invited her to shop with us, but Gwendolyn elbowed me. I think Janet saw it because she said she had to get home. I watched her walk away and go into another store, though. I told Gwendolyn she was rude. Helen says we can't be too careful. Janet's Japanese. I said she's Japanese American. Gwendolyn said I didn't understand what's going on in the world. I understand fine. But so what if her family is Japanese? She can't help that. Does that make her the enemy? Is she going to spy on us while we shop for Christmas presents and report us to the Japanese Emperor? I don't think so.

We ate dinner at the Coconut Shack. Gwendolyn's boyfriend,

Jerry, was there. They paired off to make goo-goo eyes at each other. Helen and I grabbed a booth. Later Frank and Drew came in and joined us. Drew was right across from me, so he had to talk to me! All he talked about was flying. Fine by me! Drew takes flight lessons from Mr. Tyce, the manager of the John Rodgers Airport. His father wanted him to learn from the best.

Drew said, "I saw you signed up for the aviation course, but then changed your mind."

"No way. I want to take that course more than anything, but the school may not let me." Then I told him about talking to Mr. Lindstrom. "The trouble is, I'm not sure I did well enough on the math final to make it into the class."

"I wish I'd known that. I could've helped you. Math comes easy for me."

Gosh, he's a nice guy. He's wanted to fly since he was four, when his father took him up in a plane. His mother strapped him in with tape. She was worried his father would do a roll or a spin just for fun and Drew would fall out! I told Drew the only airplane I'd ever been in was the Clipper Ship that got me to Hawaii, but that I've wanted to fly since I was eleven. That was when I saw my first barnstorming show in Florida when Dad was stationed at Pensacola. The show featured a girl pilot. She couldn't have been more than sixteen or seventeen. Somehow then I knew that was what I wanted to do.

"Wing walk?" Drew laughed.

"Well, maybe not that kind of flying. But I sure do want to learn to fly a Piper Cub."

"Hey, that's what I'm learning on. It's a great plane." He seemed surprised I knew the kind of airplane I wanted to fly. If he only saw my scrapbook!

Frank suggested we watch Drew fly sometime. Drew broke out in a huge grin. "That'd be swell. Then Ace here can see her Piper Cub." I'm sure I blushed, but I did like the way Drew called me Ace.

We haven't seen your father yet. If he gets here by Christmas, we'll make sure he spends it with us. It's got to be as hard on him as it is on you.

Your friend,

Merrie

Warm Springs, Georgia

DECEMBER 25, 1940

Dear Merrie,

Merry Christmas, Merrie! Did you ever notice how funny that looks?

I got out of my foul mood by the time the train got to Warm Springs. I guess maybe I'm getting used to the idea. Mr. Lawson from the Warm Springs Foundation met us at the train station and told us we'd just missed the president. He was here a week ago, but just for the day. Mr. Lawson said the president should be back around Easter, and Hank could meet him then. "If the war doesn't prevent him, that is," Mr. Lawson added.

Mr. Lawson wheeled Hank down to the car and lifted him into the backseat. I felt the cold steel of his braces against my legs as Hank leaned against me to see out. I hate those awful things. How is Hank ever going to walk with all that heavy metal holding him down?

Over the next few days, we explored every inch of the place. It used to be the Meriweather Inn with over 100 rooms and guest cottages when President Roosevelt bought it. The hot springs that feed the pool were a big attraction then and now. He came here often to swim and strengthen his own legs damaged by polio, but now that he's president, he only gets here once or twice a year.

Mom and I ate our meals with Hank, sat in on some of his treatments, and visited with the doctors on their plan for Hank. At one meeting, a physical therapist told us we'll be amazed at Hank's progress the next time we come to Warm Springs. He'll do exercises in the pool and, without having to steady himself or bear his own weight in the water, Hank will practice walking again. But that's just it. This is pretend walking in the pool. I feel like we're all lying to him, and I hate that. Who's going to tell Hank that real walking on the ground again isn't possible? The doctors told us of some of the new things they're trying here, but when I pressed one

of them about when Hank would walk again, he wouldn't answer. I still think we all should've stayed together in Norfolk. Hank could "not walk" there just as easily.

On Christmas Eve, Mom and I wheeled Hank to the chapel for services. Some patients walked in with their braces and crutches; others were wheeled in. Staff members carried some in on stretchers and set them down up front.

Hank loved the special presents we kept hidden until today. Dad sent Hank his old baseball glove to keep near him for inspiration. Mom gave him a small radio. Hank's already found out he can get the Yankees games here. I gave Hank a Lou Gehrig baseball card for his collection. Hank said to tell Gordo thanks for the Code-O-Graph. (I bet you drank a lot of Ovaltine this fall. Thanks!) Now that he can work the dials, he promises to send his Secret Squadron friend a coded message.

We joined Hank for a special Christmas Day dinner with all the other staff and patients. As I looked around the room at the smiles on their faces as they sang Christmas carols, I realize I have to let this go — my anger, my fear at what will happen to Hank without me. I've got to trust God that he'll take care of Hank. But can I do it? Really? Maybe this is the right place for Hank. We leave on the morning train for Washington. I just hope that's the right place for me.

Your friend,

Catherine

Pearl Harbor, Hawaii

DECEMBER 28, 1940

Dear Catherine,

Your father had to work on Christmas morning, but we snagged him for a late Christmas dinner. He looks great in the Hawaiian shirt my parents got him. I gave him a picture frame I made, and guess whose picture I put in there? He liked it a lot and said it made you seem closer at Christmas.

We watched Drew solo today. Mr. Tyce stood by with his clipboard while Drew conducted the preflight inspection of the Cub. Drew walked around the plane inspecting this and that as if he were a real pro. Frank introduced us to Drew's parents. They seem really nice, and so proud of Drew flying. I wish my parents were like that with me.

Some of his father's pilot buddies from the Army Air Corps were there to cheer Drew on. I was dying to ask the pilots about Captain Midnight, and especially what they thought of his crew member, Joyce, who, besides her superhuman eyesight, had a flair for flying. In the hopes of a future friendship with Drew, I kept my mouth shut.

Drew climbed into the cockpit and gave Mr. Tyce the thumbs-up sign. Mr. Tyce spun the propeller. Drew turned the ignition, and the engine revved up. The wind rushed past us when the plane taxied down the gravel runway and then began to pull up into the sky. There's something magical about watching that machine take off the ground and float in the air. It turned and circled at Drew's command. We watched until Drew was out of sight and cheered when he returned and made his approach to the runway.

After Drew taxied the plane to a stop, he jumped out and raised his fist in the air, shouting, "Whoa!" His father slapped him on the back and called him "Ace." His father's friends congratulated him and said, "Welcome to the Secret Squadron." *Oh my gosh, that's Captain Midnight's buddies*! Frank congratulated him, wanting to know when he was going to shoot down a German. Helen hugged him, and I stood by until the end.

I started to say something, but then Drew's father put his arm around his shoulder and steered him toward the hangar. Drew threw his goggles up in the air, and his father caught them and twirled them around. Drew grabbed the goggles and slung his arm around his father's shoulder. Drew's father called out to all the kids from school, "Coca-Colas on me. Come on." As I watched them walk away, I ached to have my mother and father feel that way about my dream.

You know what my parents said the last time I asked for flying lessons. Too expensive. Too dangerous. After today, I've got to try again. Maybe if they talked to Drew's parents. You're good at this. You always think things through rather than being so impulsive, like me. What do you think I should do? I've got to learn to fly!

Your friend,

Merrie

Washington, D.C.

JANUARY 5, 1941

Dear Merrie,

Mom's not sure when we can see Hank again. She keeps a Mason jar in the kitchen window of our new apartment here on Cathedral Avenue. Every night, she empties the change from her pocketbook into it. She calls it her Hank Fund. When we have enough money for two round-trip train tickets, we'll visit Hank.

We'd been here only one day when Mom and I took the trolley to Western High School to register. Western High is huge—some 1,500 students. That's enough kids that I should fade into the background easily. The secretary in the office looked at my report card and said I should do quite well here. I asked her about the school newspaper. She said it's very competitive, but that I ought to be able to proofread or sell subscriptions at least. I really want to be a reporter though.

The secretary gave me several editions from last semester of the *Breeze*, the school newspaper. I stayed up late reading them to learn as much as I can about Western High. The school colors are red and white. The principal's name is Dr. Newton. Everyone wants to go to the Cadet Hop. According to the paper, dream dresses are miraculous things. These dresses are made of "tulle, yards and yards of it, white or gold, pink or blue, sequin-encrusted bodice, which brings out the stars in your hair." It must cost a lot of money, this looking good for the Cadets. Speaking of the Cadets, boy oh boy, are they important. Just as important, if not more so, than the football team. Maybe it'll seem more like the Navy here after all.

The biggest event of the past few months, though, was a decision to integrate the school cafeteria. That's right. Western High voted overwhelmingly to let the boys and girls eat lunch together. After fifty years of separate lunches! Imagine that.

The *Breeze* doesn't have much news about the war in

Britain—even with the German bombing going on for months there. In fact, there isn't much news about current events at all. I read these issues cover to cover and didn't see one word about President Roosevelt's election to a third term. Never happened before, but not one mention of it in the school paper. Nothing on the debate in America about whether or not we should help England, while Germany bombs London. Nothing about the need for America to be prepared. Surprising for a school newspaper in the heart of the nation's capital, don't you think?

They definitely need me to be a reporter on this paper. I've clipped articles to drop off at the *Breeze* office. Once they read what I wrote on important current events for our old paper and an article I wrote about President Roosevelt's speech last week, I'm sure they'll want me on staff.

Sometimes I feel strange. No one else my age that I know thinks like me. I know I'm a serious person. I think hard about these things, and I'm stirred up to pray for the future of our country and the world. I feel strangely out of my own time, like I was born an adult. I know I should have more fun. I just don't know how. Everything's been so serious in my life these last two years. When you were around, you created the fun. I wish I was in Hawaii with you. Give Daddy a hug for me!

Your friend,

Catherine

Pearl Harbor, Hawaii

January 6, 1941

Dear Catherine,

The aviation course started today, without me in it. I made a B- in Math. B- and they wouldn't let me in. When I got my report card, I stared at the B-, willing it to turn into a B. What's the big difference between a B and a B-? At lunch, I hurried to the school office. Oh, no, I thought, Mrs. Hatchet's on duty.

"Sorry, girlie. Better luck next year," she said as soon as I entered the office.

"But I pulled my math grade up from a C- to a B-, and in just one test too. Isn't that good enough?"

"No, young lady. And that ought to teach you a lesson. Study harder this semester. And remember, rules are rules." She sniffed and turned back to her filing.

Rules are rules? Rules are silly and stupid and meant to be broken. I wanted to kick her stupid desk. No school rule's going to keep me from my dream.

Your friend,

Merrie

Washington, D.C.

JANUARY 6, 1941

Dear Merrie,

My first day of school at Western was a dismal failure. I couldn't find my classes before the bell rang. When I came in late, everyone stared at me. The teacher made me stand, introduce myself to the class, and tell them a little bit about myself. I blurted out, "My name's Catherine Clark. I moved here from Norfolk, Virginia, last week. I'm sixteen," and sat down as fast as possible.

No one sat with me at lunch. Having a coed lunch doesn't make any difference. The boys sit together on one side while the girls sit together on the other! The girls here are infinitely more stylish than our friends in Norfolk. I couldn't help noticing how ragged my sweater is by comparison.

I had only a few minutes after the final bell before I needed to catch the trolley for home. I ran up to the *Breeze* office on the second floor. Several students huddled together over copy and didn't even notice I'd entered the room. I cleared my throat. When a girl looked up, I told her I was new to the school, and I used to write articles for my old school newspaper in Norfolk. She said that the *Breeze* didn't have any openings for reporters, but I could proof or sell subscriptions. Just like the school secretary told me.

I bit my tongue and said I'd be back on Thursday for the meeting with the sales team. Once they read my articles, I'm sure they'll change their minds. When I got off at my trolley stop, I hoped Mom had a better first day at her new job than I had at my new school.

When Mom came in, she pulled some pennies, nickels, and dimes out of her pocketbook for the Hank Fund. As the money clinked into the jar, she asked me how it went at school. "Fine." I gave her a phony smile. I didn't want her to know how miserable it was. "How was your day, Mom?"

"Fine," she replied. Hmmm ... Fine? I wondered if her day was like mine.

As we opened a can of soup, I found out her day was not one whit like mine. Mom's one of several secretaries who sort and answer the First Lady's mail. Mom said she was in the middle of sorting the donation request letters, when the First Lady herself came into the office! She spoke with her personal secretary, Mrs. Thompson, for a few moments, then turned to introduce herself to Mom. She asked how her first day was going and welcomed her to the important job of responding to the many Americans with concerns. In a flash, she was gone again.

Mom stood there spellbound. Mrs. Thompson said, "Mrs. R's like that. She's really glad you're here." Mom said that after seeing all the mail that had to be sorted and answered, she understands why.

A few hours later, Mrs. Thompson suggested she leave work early to go with Mrs. R's staff to the gallery of the House of Representatives to hear President Roosevelt deliver his State of the Union Address. Oh, what I would've given to have been Mom today!

Mom brought home a copy of President Roosevelt's speech. President Roosevelt urged us to build a world founded upon four essential human freedoms. I can almost hear his booming voice as he said:

The first is freedom of speech and expression ... everywhere in the world.

The second is freedom of every person to worship God in his own way ... everywhere in the world.

The third is freedom from want ... everywhere in the world.

The fourth is freedom from fear ... anywhere in the world.

I rushed through my dinner so I could write my article about these democratic freedoms. It's a good article. Here's a copy for you. After I polish it, I'm going to take it to the *Breeze*. I hope it'll get published.

Your friend,

Catherine

Pearl Harbor, Hawaii

JANUARY 11, 1941

Dear Catherine,

Don't be so serious! You're right — not all teenagers are as serious-minded as you. You should go to the school dances. Have some fun. Maybe the Western High kids read all that current event stuff in the newspapers their parents have at home. Or maybe (like us), they hear the talk at the dinner table every night. Maybe the Western kids just want to enjoy their activities — the dances, the football or basketball games, the Cadet competitions, the latest fashion news, and movies and ice skating and parties. What's so wrong with that?

My challenge to you at this new school is to have fun! Meet some new friends. Enjoy some school clubs, maybe even some social ones this time. Of course, I know you'll study hard, join the History Club, make all *A*s, and win essay contests. You've always done that. But you're a sophomore now. Don't hide behind your pen all the time!

Listen to me. Giving you advice like getting what we want is easy. It's not. It's been killing me to watch the kids go to the aviation course, while I learn about how white bread is enriched with vitamins and minerals. One day I was sitting in the nutrition course, daydreaming about flying as usual, when The Plan hit me. I couldn't wait until the class was over. I took the stairs two at a time to the school newspaper office where the only typewriter in the whole school is. I asked if I could borrow it and pounded out my letter. I slid down the banister railing and raced to the school office. Mrs. Hatchet rolled her eyes when I came in. I put the letter in the principal's mailbox and rushed out again, without saying a word to that mean old bat.

There was no one to play tennis with this afternoon, but I didn't care. I couldn't concentrate anyway. I slammed the backboard over and over again. With each serve, I repeated, "This has to work."

I've asked if I can take the aviation course for no credit. Then

their stupid rule won't matter. What's one more body in a classroom? And then the school can say that there are no girls taking aviation. They can be happy, and so can I. I just want to learn. Who cares about a stupid credit? It's so frustrating. My parents won't let me take flying lessons. If the school won't let me study aviation, then I'm just left clipping articles for a scrapbook. This has to work.

Your friend,

Merrie

Washington, D.C.

January 17, 1941

Dear Merrie,

I got your letter about watching Drew solo. That must've been incredible to see, and I know you're itching to be up there too. Okay, here's what I think. Don't just beg for the lessons (your usual style). Show some responsibility about it first. Trying to get into the aviation course is a good start.

When I told Mom that you're interested in taking flying lessons, she asked me if you wanted to be a military pilot one day. That seemed absurd, but listen to this. A few months ago, Jackie Cochran wrote Mrs. Roosevelt to ask if the Air Corps would use women to ferry planes for the military like they do in England. You'd think they'd listen to her; she's broken so many records as a woman pilot. Mrs. Roosevelt believes women can do all kinds of jobs so she suggested the idea and it was shot down—for now.

Guess what else Mom told me? A lot of colleges have the Civilian Pilot Training Program. It's mostly for boys, but they do allow one college girl to be trained for every ten boys. The program pays for the flight time! Maybe if your parents see how you can continue your flying in college, then they'll be more open to it.

The *Breeze* came out today. I put a copy in here for you. My favorite article is the interview with two boys from England who go to Western now. One boy said he's confused why we salute the flag the way we do. I wish the interviewer had asked him why.

I took my "Four Freedoms" article to the *Breeze* office, and asked Jean, the assistant editor, to read it. She said the next few issues have already been planned out. How you can plan out "news"? Seems to me there should be some flexibility for some good news stories to be slipped in here or there. She took my article and the folder of the stories I wrote for our old school newspaper. She said she'd read them, but I could tell by her face, I'll be lucky if she even looks at them. I wish they'd give me a chance.

After school, some girls from my English class were on their way to the Hot Shoppes to get Coca-Colas. I heard them talking about the upcoming dance, the Cadet Hop, and who they wanted to go with. They walked by me like I wasn't even there.

I miss you. I miss Hank. I miss Daddy. And I don't feel like I fit in here at all.

Your friend,

Catherine

Pearl Harbor, Hawaii

JANUARY 26, 1941

Dear Catherine,

It worked! Mr. Lindstrom said it's fine for me to sit in on his class. He'll even let me take the tests if I want to see how I'm doing, even though they can't count toward credit. Bless you, Mr. Lindstrom!

The class has been going on for two and a half weeks already. Mr. Lindstrom gave me a copy of the book. I stayed up late for an entire week trying to catch up. Drew spent his last six lunches going over the parts I've missed so far. Helen thinks he's sweet on me. If so, he sure doesn't show it. Besides, Gwendolyn told me he's taking Patty to the tea dance at the Royal Hawaiian Saturday. That hurt.

Mother's thrilled I'm taking nutrition. I told Gordo to drink his milk the other night because it's got calcium for his bones. You should've seen the pleased look on Mother's face. I don't want to encourage her about this nursing business though. It's flying I want to do.

This week Mr. Lindstrom took the class to John Rodgers Airport to see a Piper Cub on the ground, instead of just in pictures in the book. I love this class!

Miss Guild's the one who demonstrated it to us. She's so pretty. Some of the boys whistled when she walked out of the hangar. Mr. Lindstrom jumped on them. "Young men, you're looking at a very accomplished pilot who's logged more hours in her teen years than you'll ever hope to do. Show some respect, or I'll have you booted out of this class." You should've seen their eyes bug out when they heard that!

Do you know what she told us? Five years ago, she met Amelia Earhart! Right here in Honolulu. The day before her solo flight across the Pacific Ocean to California. Mr. Lindstrom asked Miss Guild a question I know he knew the answer to, but my guess is he

wanted the boys to hear it. "Miss Guild, when Amelia Earhart flew from Honolulu to California without stopping, had any man done that before?"

"No, sir! Never done before—man or woman." Miss Guild continued to list the records broken by Amelia Earhart. Some of the boys rolled their eyes, but Drew winked at me.

Drew comes to this airport a lot to get in as much flying time as he can, and he knows how good a pilot Miss Guild is.

I was so excited when I got home. I told Mother all about it. She said she's worried taking this class is only going to make me want to fly more. Of course it will. But taking nutrition sure isn't going to make me want to be a nurse! It hurts that Mother can't see—or doesn't want to see—what this means to me.

Your friend,

Mettie

Washington, D.C.

Dear Merrie,

Every time I looked at Jean in the *Breeze* office today, I wondered if she'd read my articles and what she thought of them. Finally, after an hour of proofing some silly article about fashion, I couldn't stand it any longer. "Jean," I stammered, "have you had a chance to look at my articles yet?"

"Gee, I've been so busy with the paper and all ... well, I did take a quick look. Your writing's good. It's just that we don't have any room for these articles. Why don't you write about something going on at the school? The kids don't want to read the same stories they read at home in the *Herald* or the *Post*."

My newest article about the president's inauguration entitled "Sacrifice for Liberty" felt like a rock in my pocket. I didn't hand it in. What difference would it make?

"Will do," I said, as cheerily as possible, when she told me to write about something happening here. Inside I was furious. Write about this stupid stuff? Listen to this article in the issue of the *Breeze* I brought home today: "Advice to Girls on the Right Technique to Use with Boys."

"The first thing to do is size up your prospect. Is he the strong caveman, the quick-witted party boy, or the silent intellectual type? The first type is more likely good-looking and has had too many females tell him how wonderful he is. The surest way to trap this type is to flatter his ego."

Want more, Merrie? Well, if this guy isn't your type, here goes:

"Then there is the quick-witted party boy type who is probably the most fun of all. The problem is that when he is bored with your particular kind of sparkle, he'll be searching for another girl."

And the third type? This type might appeal to me, but I sure wouldn't interest him this way!

"The silent intellectual type in the end proves to be the true pot of gold. To interest him you must appear to be the sweet, angelic, but not-so-dumb type. None of this glamour stuff. You must appeal to him as a companion, avidly interested in things that interest him. If he likes bowling, then learn to bowl if it kills you. If he is interested in diesel engines, get a book on the darn things and at least try to look intelligent when he explains to sweet little you how they work. For heaven's sake, look impressed when he gets through, even if you knew all about them before he did."

Nope. That's not for me. I want to cover real news. I was leaving to catch the trolley when Jean said, "Hey, would you like to cover the President's Birthday Ball? I can't have you write the article because that's assigned to Linda and Robert. You could go with them, though, and provide some of the background for the piece." I jumped at the chance, and Jean gave me the ticket to the Ball and a press pass.

A press pass, Merrie! And I'm going to a dance the way I like it—with no boys. That's right. No cavemen, no quick-witted party boys, and not even the silent intellectual type. Just me and my press pass!

Your friend,

Catherine

Pearl Harbor, Hawaii

JANUARY 30, 1941

Dear Catherine,

I played tennis with Gwendolyn today. Then we went to her house. The radio was blaring in Japanese. Gwendolyn rushed to the radio and turned it off. Her mother's maid came into the living room, made small bows toward Gwendolyn, and repeated, "Sorry. Sorry."

Gwendolyn snapped, "Iced tea. With mint." The maid rushed to the kitchen, her wooden getas clacking against the floor.

"See, I told you they're not Americans. They won't even learn the language."

"Janet speaks English."

"Well, maybe to you, but not at Tokyo High or at home, I bet. Besides, those kids are just studying English to take over the positions that Americans are supposed to have."

That all sounded very much like Gwendolyn's mother to me. But you know what they say, the apple doesn't fall far from the tree. The maid returned with two tall glasses of iced tea with sprigs of green mint in them. I looked her in the eye and said, "Thank you." She kept her head bent over, wouldn't look at us, and nodded as she backed out towards the kitchen.

"Excuse me," I said, not wanting her to leave.

"Yes, Miss. More mint?"

"No. I was wondering, what's your name?"

She replied softly, "Mrs. Kawaguchi."

"I'm pleased to meet you, Mrs. Kawaguchi. That's a lovely kimono you're wearing." I stood and offered my hand. Gwendolyn groaned. Mrs. Kawaguchi touched the smooth silk of her kimono. Then she walked away, silent except for the clacking of her wooden getas.

"Really, Merrie!" chided Gwendolyn. "She's our servant. And

you're not helping. She already takes advantage of us. Uses our radio when we're gone, and who knows what else."

I realized I was in her home and shouldn't push it any further. But the next time, I'm not going to put up with Gwendolyn's snobbishness.

Your friend,

Merrie

Washington, D.C.

Dear Merrie,

It was incredible! I felt like a real reporter at the President's Birthday Ball! I put on my nicest dress and comfortable shoes. I wanted to be able to walk around all night to get information for the article on the Birthday Ball. I stuffed my hands in my pockets to keep warm on the way to the school. I turned my press card over and over in my pocket as I walked. With each turn, I thought, *This is it. I'm really going to get into a swanky place I have no business going to otherwise. All because of this card. My press card.*

I met Linda and Robert at the school, and we took the trolley together to the Earle Theater to meet some of Hollywood's stars and starlets. We interviewed Red Skelton! He's the master of ceremonies for the Ball tonight. He was easy to talk to and kept us laughing for so long with his jokes and puns that we were late to the hotel.

The lobby of the Mayflower Hotel was crowded with stars and dignitaries. We checked our coats and made our way to the East Room where the food was. Robert piled his plate high. Linda picked at a dessert on her plate, but I was too excited to eat. Lights were low, but a glittering ball hung from the ceiling reflecting speckled light across the dance floor while the orchestra played. The women wore long, shimmering gowns under thick fur coats, and the men wore their dress uniforms or tuxedos.

Linda and Robert rushed to get the autographs of Lana Turner, Maureen O'Hara, George Raft, and Wayne Morris. I took notes on the stars and starlets, but it was Mrs. Roosevelt I wanted to see. She was making the rounds tonight of the five hotels where the dances were.

Later Robert asked me to dance. My cheeks burned, and I told him maybe later. I said I needed to get a few more notes. As I hurried away, he took Linda out on the dance floor. I pretended to

take more notes, but watched him and Linda. He's a great dancer. I'm even more glad I said no because I'd just make a fool out of myself. He can even do the scissor kick when he jitterbugs.

At the end of the evening, the president's voice on the radio filled the ballroom. He thanked everyone for their help to raise money for polio research. Then he reminded everyone that because of our democratic ideals, America insists "on the right of the helpless, the right of the weak, and the right of the crippled everywhere to play their part in life — and survive." Right after his speech, a huge cake, blazing with candles, was rolled to the center of the ballroom as we sang "Happy Birthday" to the president.

Jean complimented my reporter's notes. She said they give "color" to the reporter's articles. I'd never heard that term before. She especially liked that I included information about polio, the whole reason for the Birthday Balls in the first place. Of course, I know all this from Hank. Who knows, maybe I'll submit another article after all.

Your friend,

Catherine

Pearl Harbor, Hawaii

February 15, 1941

Dear Catherine,

The Valentine's Day dance was last night. I went with Jim Reynolds, a junior. He lives here on base. He's a nice guy and all, and I had a good time. I spent more time than I'd like to admit, though, looking for Drew. I didn't see him there. And Patty was there with another boy. In a way, I was relieved. Maybe his true love is flying after all!

Tell your mom that Jackie Cochran was named the best woman pilot for three years straight. Those big shots in Washington should pay attention to her. Let me know if you hear anything else about the women ferrying planes idea. I've got to come up with reasons for Mother to see that aviation for women is the way of the future. Otherwise, it's nursing school for me, and a life filled with bandages, germs, and sick people. Ugh.

I asked your father to take me to see the seaplanes at Kaneohe. These planes are huge! These Navy planes hunt for enemy submarines. Hmmm ... sounds like Captain Midnight again.

Three of the planes came in from patrol and landed as smooth as silk on the water at the end of the island. They have no wheels, so your father showed me how they get the planes on a trailer to get them into the hangar. We followed one of these planes inside, where the pilot let me get in the cockpit. Whoa, was I up high off the ground!

I asked a ton of questions. The young (and very handsome) lieutenant said he was surprised how much I knew. I confessed I'd been reading about flying and knew some basic questions to ask. Your father kidded me and said, "Hey, Meredith, who knows? Maybe one day, you'll be a Navy pilot!"

The young lieutenant, who can't be but a few years older than me, said, "Girl Navy pilots. That'll be the day." He laughed so hard, it made me furious. "Besides, even if they did let them in, they'd wash out the first week." Oh, that got my blood boiling. I'll show them all!

Your friend,

Merrie

Pearl Harbor, Hawaii

FEBRUARY 23, 1941

Dear Catherine,

Gwendolyn and I played tennis again. She's getting better, but she's still no match for you. We're going to enter a doubles tournament anyway. If you were here, we'd wipe up the court. After our game, we went to her house for iced tea. I said hello to Mrs. Kawaguchi. She smiled back this time. Gwendolyn rolled her eyes, but I noticed the radio was playing nice Hawaiian music on an English-speaking channel.

We drank our tea and talked about school. That's when she asked me if I liked Drew. I guess it shows. I told her I think he's a great guy, but that he's got only one thing on his mind and that's flying. She said if I'd stop this silly idea about trying to be one of the boys, then maybe the boy I like would pay more attention.

"Really, Merrie, you could use a little help." She sat me down in front of her dressing table and undid my ponytail. "You can be pretty when you try, you know."

I felt like one of the girls in your fashion column. For the next half hour, Gwendolyn tried three different hairstyles on me, made me try on her clothes, and showed me how to put on lipstick. When she was satisfied with the new me, she said, "Now Drew will notice." I looked in the mirror but didn't recognize the person who looked back. I had to admit I looked pretty. Maybe I should wear my hair down more often. And that shade of lipstick did look good on me.

I decided to let Gwendolyn in on my secret. I told her I wanted to learn to fly. She said, "And wear coveralls and have grease all over your face? You've got to be kidding. Do you want Drew as your boyfriend or not? If it's a friend you want, then go ahead and keep this silly idea of flying. But if you want him to be your boyfriend, then be interested in flying, but you don't have to learn to fly to do that. You don't see me playing football, do you? But

after every game, I tell Jerry what a great play he made. I don't have to understand the mechanics of the play. I just tell him how good he looked when he caught that ball."

On the way home, I thought about what she said. I can't picture myself oohing and cooing over Drew's turns and spins, and not wanting to do those myself. I think if Drew doesn't like a girl who wants to fly, then he's not the boy for me anyway. I fingered the new lipstick Gwendolyn gave me that was in my skirt pocket. It is a nice color on me, and I like being pretty. And Drew's been nice enough, but he hasn't asked me out. I wonder if Gwendolyn's right?

Gordo whistled when I came home. He said he likes my hair better this way. Geez, Louise. A compliment from my kid brother.

Your friend,

Merrie

Washington, D.C.

MARCH 4, 1941

Dear Merrie,

There was a huge snowstorm for the Cadet Hop on Friday. I didn't go, but Margaret did and she told me it was a lot of fun. The eight inches of snow didn't keep the gym from hopping until midnight. I asked her if she saw Robert. She said he was one of the best dancers there. Ouch. I have no chance with someone like that.

I heard from Hank today. He's trying crutches, but his arm strength isn't good enough yet for him to stand on his own. The best I can hope for is that Hank can stand, but he still believes he's going to walk again.

Hank's excited about baseball season starting soon. He won't miss one of those Yankees games, but he sure does miss Lou Gehrig from the lineup. It's a shame he had to stop playing. At Christmas when I gave Hank the Lou Gehrig baseball card, Hank reminded me that the doctors at first thought Mr. Gehrig had polio. It wasn't, but his disease continues to attack his muscles. Lou Gehrig's courage, both on and off the field, inspires Hank. He used to tell me, "If the Iron Horse can handle his disease, then I can handle this iron lung."

Today at the *Breeze* office, I turned in my latest proofing assignment. Jean asked me if I'd like to try my hand at editing an article. Would I? You bet!

I practically flew home. I couldn't wait until Mom got home to show her. By the time she'd arrived, I had read the article six times and thought about what edits I wanted to make. I didn't dare make any pencil marks yet. Not until I'm sure what I think. I had to write to you first, and then Hank. Maybe I'm afraid. What if my editing isn't good enough?

I can't think about that now. I'm not going to blow this chance to show Jean I can do more than proofing.

Your friend,

Catherine

Pearl Harbor, Hawaii

March 6, 1941

Dear Catherine,

I know, you're going to say, "I told you so." It probably wasn't the best time to ask them about flying lessons, but I just couldn't take it any longer. I felt like I was going to burst, and it all just spilled out. The Clipper ride. Watching Drew solo. Auditing the school aviation class. Getting all As on the tests that I volunteered to take even though they don't count for credit. All the "how to fly" instruction books tucked under my bed. Sitting in the cockpit of the sea patrol plane. My request for flight lessons.

They didn't say a word at first. Then they gave each other "the look." Dad got up and said he had to leave. Mother said, "Merrie, your father has to leave." No kidding. As she walked Dad to the door, he turned, and said, "Meredith, we'll talk about this later."

Uh-oh. He said "Meredith." That's his "this is serious, young lady" name for me. Mother gave me the "don't you dare ask me to give my opinion until your father and I have talked about this" look. I can tell from their faces it doesn't look good. Why can't they see how much this means to me? Don't they understand I don't want to be them? I want to follow my own dreams. If only they'd give me their decision. The suspense is killing me. My whole future is in their hands, and I'm scared.

Your friend,

Merrie

Washington, D.C.

MARCH 7, 1941

Dear Merrie,

Margaret and I went to Hot Shoppes after school today. The waitress brought us our usual Coca-Cola with two straws. They cost seven cents, and I can't afford a whole one. I only took a few sips. Margaret tells me not to worry. She's sure that Jean will like what I've done. I'm trying not to be anxious, but it's been three long days since I've turned it in. Jean hasn't said anything about it. She probably hates it.

We got a letter from Daddy today. He's joined a Navigators group that meets in Honolulu. He said he keeps his mind busy learning new Scriptures. I didn't think Daddy could learn any more Scriptures. Daddy challenged me and Hank to memorize the same Scriptures with him. He sent me a card with a verse on it, and said he's sending the same card to Hank. This will make it fun, and maybe we'll all feel closer.

I'm so sorry it didn't go over well with your parents. You've got to admit that it's a bit unusual for a sixteen-year-old girl to get her private pilot's license. Mom told me there are about a thousand girls and women who have their pilot's license, some as young as fifteen. But most of those girls live on farms with wide-open spaces to land in the fields, practice turns, and do maneuvers. You're there in the middle of one of the largest military buildups in history. There are Navy and Air Corps pilots up in the sky all day long. Daddy wrote to us that, even on Sunday mornings, there are drills and maneuvers with the Air Corps guys trying to out-buzz the Navy pilots.

As the daughter of a naval officer, one day you're supposed to put on your fancy hat, white gloves, and go with your naval officer husband to call on the other naval officer families. The idea you'd put on pants and goggles and take off into the sky instead just

doesn't fit with Navy life. In the life we know, what you're asking is just not done.

I'm sure your parents don't see a future in it for you. Didn't you tell me your mom has been trying to get you to join the Junior Red Cross there and learn first aid? You know she wants you to follow in her footsteps. My advice? Take it slow. Let them think it over for a while, and for heaven's sake, Merrie, DON'T PUSH!!

Your friend,

Catherine

Washington, D.C.

Dear Merrie,

This afternoon, I picked up the latest issue of the *Breeze*. It was hard to open the paper because my hands were shaking. I quickly scanned the paper looking for the article I'd edited. I read it as fast as I could. I read it again. I couldn't believe it.

No changes, Merrie! Not a single change made to the article as I edited it. All my suggestions, revisions, and edits were accepted! I took the steps two at a time up to the *Breeze* office.

Jean smiled at me when I walked in and said, "So, how does it feel?" I was thrilled and told her so. Jean said, "Your work's good. It's just that the articles you like to write are too serious for this paper. The kids want to read about what interests them. You're more serious-minded than most kids."

"I know," I replied. "I've heard that before."

"To make a school newspaper successful, you have to provide articles of interest to the majority of the students. Like the column in the school paper on fashion." I groaned inwardly as she picked up today's issue and read, "National defense has influenced fashion greatly this spring. Clothes have gone *tres militaire* and the predominating colors are red, white, and blue."

"Well, at least they mentioned national defense," I said weakly.

Jean laughed and then told me horrible news. "I'm resigning from the *Breeze* at the end of the month," she said. "My uncle runs a newspaper in Georgetown, and I'll work for him after school."

Just when I've won the respect of the assistant editor, she's leaving. I don't know the editor-in-chief very well. "That's wonderful," I said, but not with much enthusiasm.

"I spoke with Bill, and he's willing to move Robert up to assistant editor, and give you Robert's position as a reporter. But be prepared. Most of what you'll report on as the junior staff member will be the social events and human interest stories. I think the closest you'll get to news about the defense of America is what we just read in the fashion column."

Jean also asked me if I'd be interested in a paid position on her uncle's newspaper two afternoons a week as a copy girl. Would I? You bet! She'll set up an interview with her uncle, Mr. McGurdy, next week. "When I heard how you were dressed for the Birthday Ball, I knew you'd be right for this position," she added.

I had worn a very nice dress, but my shoes were definitely not the kind the fashion column would recommend. They were for scouting out news, not dancing the lindy. My face burned as I realized that Robert or Linda must have told her about them.

"Don't be embarrassed," Jean continued. "It was just one more thing that made me think of you when my uncle asked if I knew any possibilities for copy boys or copy girls. You came to mind because of those shoes, not in spite of them."

Jean explained that the way reporters often turn stories in is not at all like what it is here at the *Breeze*. The reporter might send up an article to the editor's desk a page at a time. The reporter yells, "Copy!" Then the copy girl rushes over, grabs the page he has just pulled out of his typewriter, and runs that page up to the editorial desk. After the editor has reviewed all the pages and made his edits, then the copy girl takes the copy pages and pastes the article together page by page. After it's all pasted together, the copy girl takes the article to the composing room.

My eyes got bigger and bigger as she spoke. I could almost smell the ink from the presses and the hot coffee and hear the voices of reporters yelling out, "Copy!" And, "Send me that copy girl, Catherine. She's fast."

"Catherine? Catherine, are you listening?"

"Sorry, I was just imagining what it'd be like."

"Well, it's not very glamorous. There're lots of chores too. You might refill paste pots, sweep up, or get coffee for anyone who wants

it. Basically, you're there to do whatever's needed, whenever it's needed."

That didn't change my mind. I told Jean I'd love this job. She told me that she couldn't promise it to me. I'd have to meet her uncle first. She smiled and added, "But I'll recommend you highly. You and your shoes."

Tonight is the first night I went to bed actually glad we moved.

Your friend,

Catherine

Washington, D.C.

MARCH 21, 1941

Dear Merrie,

This afternoon after school, I took the trolley to the *Georgetown Chronicle* office. I wore my nicest skirt and blouse and my dependable shoes. If he hired me on the spot and wanted me to work that day, I was ready.

The receptionist had me wait in the lobby for fifteen minutes. I took in every detail. I could smell the printer's ink and hear the jangle of the telephones, the clicking of the typewriter keys, and the presses pounding in the basement. A booming voice yelled out, "Copy!" I closed my eyes and imagined I was the one who snatched the page from the reporter and rushed it up to Mr. McGurdy's desk. What would he look like? Would he be tall, wear a nice suit, and have a pen in his hand, ever ready to correct an article?

The receptionist, Miss Gladstone, showed me into his office, which was filled with smoke. There stood Mr. McGurdy with shirtsleeves rolled up, hair every which way, cigar wagging in his mouth as he talked to his cub reporter. I waited while he scolded this reporter for not checking his source. Mr. McGurdy wadded up the article and threw it in the trash. The reporter ducked out with Mr. McGurdy still ranting about youngsters and incompetence. "A high school reporter could do a better job than you!" he yelled down the hall.

I cleared my throat.

"Whaddaya want?" he grumbled.

"Mr. McGurdy, my name is Catherine Clark. I'm here about the copy girl job." He didn't seem to know who I was. I didn't want to mention Jean because I wanted to see if I could get this job on my own.

"Qualifications?"

"I was a reporter for my school paper in Norfolk. When I moved to Washington, there was no reporter job open on Western High

School's paper, the *Breeze*. Didn't stop me, sir. I signed up to do whatever I could. I sold subscriptions, proofed copy, and went on assignment at the President's Birthday Ball to get background for the reporters. I'll do the same for you. Whatever you ask, sir."

"Sold subscriptions, eh? Well, I tell you what. You start out selling subscriptions door to door, and we'll see."

My heart sank, but in a cheerful voice I said, "Yes, sir, when can I start?" He sent me out the door with a subscription pad, pencils, and a zippered pocket envelope with change in it. I didn't know where to begin, but decided the brownstone houses nearest the paper were as good a spot as any. For the next three hours, I knocked on doors and sold subscriptions.

I was bone tired when I returned. I smoothed out my hair and took the subscription pad filled with new subscriptions, and the zippered pocket envelope now stuffed with money, up to his office. Mr. McGurdy was hunched over his desk scribbling on papers as fast as he could. "Copy!" he yelled and a boy about my age rushed to grab the paper from him. Without looking up, he said, "Good job, Clark. Come back tomorrow and sell some more."

My first day on the job of a real paper and I hardly saw the inside of it. All I did was walk around neighborhoods selling subscriptions. I might as well be at the *Breeze*. I was exhausted and so disappointed. This wasn't at all what I expected. Why don't things ever turn out right?

Your friend,

Catherine

Pearl Harbor, Hawaii

MARCH 23, 1941

Dear Catherine,

Finally, two weeks after I asked my parents, they told me what they thought. The answer's no. Dad went into a long litany of everything they had done to check it out. Dad visited John Rodgers Airport and talked with Miss Guild and Mr. Andrews. He took your father with him to check out the Piper Cub trainers. Dad got information on the prices and on the requirements to get a private license, and how much flight time costs.

"Meredith," Dad said.

Uh-oh, I thought. He said "Meredith."

"Your mother and I have prayed about this a lot. We appreciate your not pushing the issue, and we know that's been hard for you. You know we want to encourage your interest; we always have."

I could feel it coming. The "but" was about to form on his lips. I tried one last valiant effort. "Before you say anything else, I've been thinking about exactly what you're talking about. I can get a job. I type fast. I can work at the commissary."

Dad said, "It's just two years until you'll go to college. Even if you get a job, we'd like you to contribute to your college savings. We just don't see how flying fits into our family's life or budget right now. "

"But," I protested, "what about my life? This is what I want more than anything. More than college!"

"We've looked into this carefully and considered all the possibilities. Your mother and I agree that the answer for now is no."

"It's not fair. I said I'd pay for the lessons. The plane's safe. I've learned ground instruction better than the boys in the class. Please, think about it some more. Don't say no yet. Just think about it."

Dad said the issue was closed, so I ran to my room and slammed the door. No need to discuss it further. They'd made that clear. "The

issue is closed." Closed for them, maybe, but not me. They have to let me grow up sometime! I don't care what they say, I'm going to find a way to fly.

Your friend,

Merrie

Washington, D.C.

APRIL 9, 1941

Dear Merrie,

For two weeks now, day after day, I've sold subscriptions to Mr. McGurdy's paper every afternoon. I've stayed up late to finish my schoolwork. My feet hurt and my legs ache. I've walked all over this town in pouring rain. I've had doors slammed in my face. You'd think by now Mr. McGurdy would let me do something else. Running copy sounds glamorous now after all this trooping around!

Every day when I return from my sales calls, I breathe in the musty smell of the printer's ink as I enter the door. The now familiar "Hello, doll" from Miss Gladstone is music to my ears. Mr. Ward, with a pencil behind his ear, never fails to smile at me and wave even as he talks on his telephone with his sources to find his next scoop. This is where I want to be. In the middle of everything. Not down the street selling subscriptions. But gruff old Mr. McGurdy seems to be warming up to me. Just yesterday, after I put the subscription slips and money on his desk as usual, he said, "Clark, you're doing good." Good at selling, maybe, but it's the news reporting I want in on. Well today, it finally happened, but not because of Mr. McGurdy.

You know how the Germans blitzed Coventry, England, all night last night? (As if Coventry can take any more after the bombing last fall.) Anyway, the phones kept ringing as reporters checked their sources to find information about the bombing—the number of casualties, the types of buildings hit, the kinds of bombs and incendiary devices, and what the British and the Americans were saying about the bombings.

I pulled off my jacket and rolled up my sleeves. I could tell this was going to be a long night. And I didn't want to miss one minute of it. I called Mom to tell her I'd be home late. Mr.

McGurdy's office was jammed with reporters. He shouted rapid-fire instructions to each of them as to what subject to cover and what angle to explore. I stayed at the edge of the door to his office and listened. "Medfield, you take the political angle; Sanders, take the casualty data; Ward, human interest; and Connors, follow up with your sources from the Hill. Gibson, I want to know everything there is about the bombs: When did they drop them? Were they exploding bombs or just to mark the targets? Details, people. Give me details. Meet back here in half an hour."

As the reporters scrambled past me, I remembered a newsreel I'd seen in the movies about the last German raids on Coventry. What stuck with me from this newsreel was the story of Warwickshire Hospital. The hospital displayed a large red cross on its roof—perfect target practice for the Germans. The Germans hit the hospital twice that night. Half of its rooms were destroyed. The hospital had no running water, electricity, or windows. Yet the doctors and nurses continued to work all night on casualties brought into the hospital. The surgeons operated without electricity. Amazingly, despite these conditions, they didn't lose one patient.

I placed the subscription slips and the money on Mr. McGurdy's desk. He didn't notice me as he pored over copy. I ran down to the newsroom and found Mr. Ward, deep in thought.

"Mr. Ward, I remembered this newsreel I saw last fall about the raid on Coventry. I wondered if you might write a story on Warwickshire Hospital. Perhaps you could compare how it came through this time with the last raid." Then I told him all I remembered from the newsreel.

Mr. Ward chewed on the end of his pencil, and said, "Hey, good idea about the hospital, kid. Thanks." About that time, Mr. Sanders yelled, "Coffee!" and I was off and running.

I got home very late, but Mom had waited up for me. She made me a glass of warm milk. I kept thinking of the copy pages I had run up to Mr. McGurdy, pasted together, and taken to the composing room. The stories poured in about the destruction of lives and homes. As the word pictures of those articles flashed across my mind, I shivered and drew closer to Mom on the sofa. She put her arms around me and asked if I knew the story of the Cathedral of St. Michael in Coventry. I shook my head.

"In last November's raid, the Germans bombed the cathedral. The fire raged throughout the night. Despite the best efforts of firemen, who stood all night throwing incendiary bombs off the roof with their spades as soon as they landed, the cathedral burned to the ground. The next morning, the stonemason and caretaker of the cathedral grounds, Jock Forbes, came to see the destruction from the horrific bombing. He spotted a pair of charred beams from the fourteenth-century roof that had fallen down, lying across each other in the rubble. He fastened them into the shape of a cross and planted it in the blackened remains of the building.

"They decided that very day to rebuild the cathedral from the rubble, not as an act of defiance, but as a sign of faith, trust, and hope for the future of the world. Two months later, the stonemason, Mr. Forbes, built the rough stone altar in the apse of the destroyed cathedral. He placed the charred cross behind it with the words inscribed on it: 'Father Forgive.'

"It's Easter this Sunday, Catherine," Mom said as she kissed me good night. "Never forget that resurrection follows death—if we trust in the Lord."

Tonight, we prayed together for the men, women, and children of Coventry.

Your friend,

Catherine

Pearl Harbor, Hawaii

APRIL 10, 1941

Dear Catherine,

Now don't scold me, but I've figured out a way to earn flight time. I'm working for Andrews Flying Service! Twice a week, while my parents think I'm at the library after school, I take the bus out to the hangar and do whatever they need me to do. I schedule appointments for tourists to go flight-seeing. I spread hot goop on the cloth wings of the planes to make them waterproof. I clean the airplane windshields. So much gunk gets on them. I stack the parachutes. Miss Guild says she can't let me learn to fold them yet, but I've been watching her and learning anyway.

For every three hours of work, Mr. Andrews will give me ten minutes of flight lessons. When Miss Guild heard about the deal I'd struck with Mr. Andrews, she told me I remind her of herself. When she was fifteen, she hitchhiked here several times each week instead of going to the beach where her parents thought she was. She worked for Mr. Andrews to earn flight time too. The only difference is as soon as she earned her flight time, she took it. She was already flying at fifteen. Her parents didn't find out until two years later. She said as much as she sympathizes with me now, there are rules now and she can't let me learn to fly without my parents' permission. Rules. Again.

But at least I'm around airplanes. And I'm logging time to spend one day for lessons. That is, if Dad and Mother ever change their minds. At least, the we don't have the money excuse will go away. I can work about six hours a week to make sure I'm home by supper. That's twenty minutes of flying time I earn a week. If only Gwendolyn could see me now. I wear coveralls. My hair's back in a ponytail, and my hands are greasy. But it's the only way.

Tonight at supper, Dad told us about a meeting he went to that day where General Short spoke about Honolulu's preparedness in case of an emergency. Everyone, military and civilians, are supposed to save up six months' supply of food. Canned goods are the best. The police are training civilians to guard utilities and prevent sabotage. It was his last point that gave me chills: they're making plans for the evacuation and shelter of women and children.

Mother told me the Germans bombed Coventry over and over again this week. She and Dad think it's a real possibility war could come to us here in Paradise. It seems so beautiful here, but there are many more planes flying maneuvers now than when we first got here. Are they doing more practice drills because they know something we don't? Could we be attacked soon? Would the Japanese bomb us here the way the Germans have bombed England? It's scary. I had to do something to get my mind off of how frightened I felt. I jumped up from the table and counted the cans in the pantry. We had six cans of soup, peas, carrots, and beans, but eleven cans of Spam. That's sure not six months' worth of rations.

Your friend,

Merrie

Washington, D.C.

April 11, 1941

Dear Merrie,

Last night, the Germans bombed Coventry again all night. How much more can the British take? Everyone's talking about it at school. Margaret made an announcement about starting a Junior Red Cross chapter to roll bandages and prepare packages for Britain. Senior boys in the cafeteria talked about which branch of the military they want to join. Everyone wants to do something. We all feel so helpless.

I stopped by the *Breeze* office yesterday to see if I had any assignments. Robert said he's missed seeing me around and asked how the job was going. When I told him all about the newsroom and the scramble to get the facts about Coventry, he said he wished he could get a job there too. His duties as squadron leader of his Cadet Corps keep him busy after school. The big competition's coming up soon. These Cadets will probably be the soldiers and sailors in our Army and Navy soon. Robert says he wants to enlist just as soon as he can.

I didn't sell subscriptions today after school. Mr. McGurdy called me into his office and said, "Clark, heard you had a good idea yesterday about a human interest piece. Why don't you follow that up with Ward today?"

Mr. Ward had me make phone calls to doctors and nurses he knew to see if they had contacts in England. After about thirty calls, I found someone who'd met a surgeon several years ago in Coventry at a summer conference. He thought he worked at Warwickshire. After a few minutes, he called us with the contact information. The surgeon lives a ways out from Coventry, but at least at the time he met him he worked at the hospital. I handed the lead to Mr. Ward and watched as he dialed the phone. Mr. Ward put his hand over the phone and said, "Lines down for the last two

days. More bombing last night." The phone rang and rang, but no one answered. "It's okay, kid. It's a good story idea. We'll keep following it up. Now take this up to the chief, please."

That was it. My brief venture into the world of reporting stopped by downed telephone lines. I spent the rest of the day running copy. News poured in all last night about the raid on Coventry, the second of this holy week. For eight long hours bombs dropped on this city I was starting to get to know. How many lives were lost last night? How many families were huddled together in bomb shelters? And how many more were lying in the rubble, injured or dead?

I'm so thankful we've never experienced anything like this. I hope and pray we never do.

Your friend,

Catherine

Washington, D.C.

APRIL 12, 1941

Dear Merrie,

I wasn't scheduled to work today, but I couldn't stay away. I asked Mom if I could go to the *Chronicle* office and help out. I smiled meekly and told her it might mean a few extra dollars for the Hank Fund.

I took the early morning trolley from Cathedral Avenue to Georgetown and walked to the newspaper office. Mr. Ward waved as I came in the door. "Hey, kid, over here," he said. "You're just in time." His desk was littered with crumpled paper, cold cups of coffee, and chewed pencils.

"Were you here all night?" I asked.

"The war isn't letting many of us sleep these days," he said. "At least not those of us that want the scoop on a certain hospital in Coventry." I pulled up a chair next to his. "Communication's been restored. I've talked to two nurses at the hospital, but our doctor friend's been in surgery for days now. In twenty minutes, I've got a phone appointment with him at his home. I'm working on my questions now."

He shoved his notes over to me, and I read what the nurse had told him. The hospital received at least ten direct hits and is totally destroyed. Doctors, nurses, and staff cared for the patients all through the night as bomb after bomb blasted the building. They searched for patients. This nurse personally saw at least ten patients who died in the raid. She started to go to the basement to the air raid shelter with the patients who could walk. The matron ordered her, as senior nurse, to go to the male medical ward instead, and sent another nurse in her place. After hours of bombing, the "all clear" signal was sounded. The patients, doctors, and nurses who had been huddled in the basement for safety started to leave. A delayed-action bomb went off, killing at least two doctors, eleven nurses, and over twenty patients. This nurse watched as they brought the bodies of Dr. Gray and Dr. Gore-Grimes, white coats covered with dirt and ash, out of the hole in the ground. Then she watched the body of Nurse Brinker carried out. That was the nurse sent in her place.

Mr. Ward's notes show he asked her if she prayed during the raid. She said she prayed the entire time and was not afraid. She was able to go about her duties with ash and cinders falling all around her. She spent as much time putting out fires caused by incendiary devices as she did caring for the patients. Through the entire night, she repeated, "Father, forgive them."

When Mr. Ward called the doctor, he tipped the earpiece of the phone and let me lean in close to hear. The search for the wounded and survivors continues in the rubble, he said. It may be weeks before they know the extent of the bombing. The doctor was treating a fireman with burns when a bomb hit with such force he was blown off the operating table. Can you believe it? The doctor was thrown to the ground with glass shattering everywhere. Amazingly, the fireman survived.

After Mr. Ward thanked the doctor, he placed the phone in the cradle gently. It was as if he were lowering a casket into holy ground on this day before Easter. May there be the promise of resurrection.

Your friend,

Catherine

Washington, D.C.

Dear Merrie,

I wish you and your family could visit us and go with us to our church, New York Avenue Presbyterian. People line up for blocks just to hear the Scottish minister, Dr. Marshall. He speaks so powerfully, and every Sunday he seems to speak just to me.

You know how heavy my heart's been this week, thinking of the British people, especially those in Coventry. Yesterday I heard the voice of the doctor crack when he told us of the devastation and loss of life. Today, I heard the strong and reassuring voice of Dr. Marshall reminding me what Easter Day is all about.

He said it'd be perfectly normal to think this whole world is hopeless. He said that reading about the air raids and the deaths of hundreds of people each night makes us think that nothing can stop the hate and violence. I pulled out my pen and pad and began to take notes. Somehow, I knew I'd want to read these notes again.

It's not hopeless … "Time and again hate has always been on the verge of winning. Yet always losing the day." To find peace, it'll take more than armies and navies. It will take the spiritual birth in the hearts and souls of people … "This is the message of Easter Day! That this changing is still possible. No matter how hopeless it appears to be, there is still hope! No matter how deep your despair has been, there is still hope!"

Mom and I had Sunday dinner with a friend of hers from the White House secretarial pool. I excused myself to walk outside while they talked. I walked by the snowflake blossoms of the cherry trees, the pink and reds and whites of the azalea bushes, and the golden sprays of wisteria blooms. I could not help but contrast that with the mental pictures I have of Coventry—charred beams, ashes and rubble, crumbled bricks, and shattered glass.

In the midst of this beauty, I prayed for God to restore my hope.

I asked him to let me learn how to trust him when circumstances shout despair and destruction. The Bible calls them "sacrifices of thanksgiving." I think I know why now. When you feel hopeless, it's a challenge to thank God. I asked God to make me like those nurses who spoke about their faith while bombs and fires rained down on them. Could I be like that if put to the test? I don't think so — not without God's help.

Your friend,

Catherine

Pearl Harbor, Hawaii

APRIL 14, 1941

Dear Catherine,

Today I painted hot goop onto the wing of a Piper Cub. The drippy mess was everywhere. On the wing, on my coveralls, on my face. Spreading the hot goop on the plane's wing made the steaming afternoon sun even hotter. I'd just about finished when I heard my name. It was Drew! "Miss Guild told me you were here."

I slid down from the airplane. Drew laughed and took his handkerchief out to wipe off the grease from my nose. Oh great, coveralls, ponytail, and no makeup except for grease. I wished I'd at least put on the new lipstick Gwendolyn had given me.

"What are you doing? Can't get enough of these airplanes in class?" He brought me a bottle of Coca-Cola. We sat down on the grass near the Cub. I pressed the cool bottle to my forehead before taking a sip.

Drew had just a few minutes before his flight time. He said he's working toward instrument ratings for bigger planes. I told Drew about the plan I had to earn money for lessons. I didn't tell Drew my parents were dead set against my flying for now.

As he stood up to leave, he said, "Hey, why don't I take you up sometime? I can take passengers now." I hesitated. He pointed to the can of goop on the grass. "It'll be better than this."

"Sounds great," I replied. And it did. But Dad and Mother would kill me. It's bad enough that I'm working here two days a week. If they found out I was up in the sky without their permission, then that's it. The end of my dream. Nope, the closest I'm going to get for now is spreading goop on the wings of the planes.

Drew asked me to spin the propeller on his plane. I had to jump up to get hold of it, but it was fun. I watched as the plane taxied down the runway and lifted off. Drew circled back and wiggled his wings. I waved back.

All the way home on the bus, I imagined what it would be like to fly. I knew my way around the Piper Cub well enough on the ground. But what's it like to feel the wind in your face and look down on the ocean and fields from high above? I leaned close to the window and felt the breeze rush past. I closed my eyes and imagined myself as a passenger in Drew's plane. Or better yet, I imagined myself at the controls of the Cub, my feet on the rudder pedals and my hand on the stick, the little plane rising and falling at my command. The bus driver whistled to get my attention at my stop.

Mother asked me what I did today to get so sunburned on my face. I didn't lie, but I didn't tell her the truth either. I don't know how much longer I can keep my working at Andrews a secret. But if I do tell them, they'll ground me for sure. Then it's no flying, no rides in planes, and not even any hot goop anymore! I'll take my chances for now.

Your friend,

Merrie

Washington, D.C.

APRIL 28, 1941

Dear Merrie,

It's been a busy couple of weeks. I've had a lot of work to do for the *Breeze*, and I spend at least three afternoons a week at the *Chronicle*. Here are some articles from both papers. You'll see the human interest story Mr. Ward wrote on the Warwickshire Hospital. He let me try my hand at proofing and editing one of his paragraphs. I want to be a crackerjack reporter one day. I'll do whatever it takes to get noticed by Mr. McGurdy — sell more subscriptions, get copy up and down to him the fastest, deliver coffee to the reporters with a smile and a sweet roll. I sharpen pencils, sweep up, and clean out paste pots. Will he ever notice? Or is it paste pot washing forever?

Hank's using crutches now! His arms are strong enough to take his weight as he stands. He's only taken a few steps and says the braces feel like bricks tied to his legs, but he's determined to walk again. I'm still upset that no one's had the nerve to tell Hank what his real chances are. How can they keep giving him false hope? Hank thinks his progress is because of the pool. He told Mom in his last letter to tell Mrs. Roosevelt to get the president down there for a swim with him. Mom wrote back that she just might do that!

Your friend,

Catherine

Pearl Harbor, Hawaii

MAY 1, 1941

Dear Catherine,

Oh boy, I've done it now. I went flying with Drew today.

For the last two weeks, every time Drew came to the airport, he'd offer to give me a ride. Each time, I had some excuse why I couldn't go. On Wednesday, he asked if I worked on Saturday, and thinking he might ask me out, I said no. "Good," he replied, "that's the day I'll take you flying." I didn't know how to get out of it. Okay, truth is, I didn't want to get out of it.

I told Mother I'd meet Helen in Honolulu for breakfast, go swimming at the beach, and then go to the movies. I took the bus to Honolulu all right, but met Drew instead. Once we were at the airport, I waited while he filled out the paperwork. I felt guilty about lying to Mother that way, but why can't they understand? I just had to know how it felt. Drew had no idea that it wasn't okay with my parents. I felt bad about that too. He's too much of a gentleman to take me up in the plane if he knew I didn't have my parents' permission.

Just when my conscience was starting to get to me, Drew came out smiling. I watched as he inspected his plane, checking off items on his clipboard. My stomach tightened and my mouth went dry. I wasn't sure whether it was from lying, or from knowing I was about to do something my folks would be furious with me about if they found out, or from the excitement of finally being able to go up in the air.

When the cross-check was over, he helped me up in the plane first, and then he jumped in. I put on the goggles Drew handed me. When I felt the wind across my face as he taxied down the runway, I forgot all about my guilty conscience.

Half an hour later, Drew circled around and brought the plane back down in a flawless landing. He helped me down from the plane. For once, I was speechless. Drew understood and didn't say a word.

Later when I was with Helen, she said I seemed sad. I was a bundle of emotions. I was thrilled to have flown, but now sorry I can't share it with anyone, especially my family. I was happy Drew had asked me to go with him, but worried that he might say something to the other kids who go to our church. What if it gets back to Mother and Dad? After all, Drew doesn't think it's a big secret.

I may have gotten myself in a whale of a mess.

Your friend,

Merrie

Washington, D.C.

Dear Merrie,

I got your letter about flying with Drew. Now I'm not going to say what you already know. But I will say this. Go tell your parents right away. Sure they'll be angry, but better it come from you than someone else. This can't be sitting well with you. Go get it straightened out. Confess, Merrie.

I see Robert at the *Breeze* more now that the competition is over. His Cadet Corps, Company K, defeated all the other high schools in the citywide competition. Margaret and I watched from the reviewing stands with thousands of students, parents, and teachers as the Western High companies took first, fourth, fifth, and sixth places.

After the competition, a lot of the kids met at the Hot Shoppes. This time Margaret convinced me to go with her. The soda fountain was jammed, and we couldn't get a table for a while. When the Cadets arrived, all the kids cheered and clapped. The boys lifted Robert and some others up on their shoulders. I couldn't help but think that these fifteen-, sixteen-, and seventeen-year-olds, so proud of their performance today, might be marching off to war in the next few years.

I went up to Robert and said hello. He seemed friendly and glad to see me. I blurted out, "Congratulations! I'm proud of you … I mean, Company K." He smiled and said, "Thanks!" See, I'm trying! I have to admit I had fun with the kids today. I felt like a part of Western High, cheering for our Cadets.

I've enclosed the latest issue of the *Breeze*, from May 6th. You can read all about Company K and see the pictures of the competition. There's a picture of Robert. We're beginning to see some changes at Western High and the *Breeze* is reporting them (finally!). The small article on page 3 talks about the new aviation

course for boys (sorry!). Robert told me he thinks this is just one step away from offering flying lessons for the boys who want to learn. "Future pilots for the war," he added.

The editorial this week, "Freedom's Cost," encourages Western students to buy defense stamps at the cafeteria. If each of the five million students in the United States donated twenty cents weekly, that'd be a total of one million dollars each week. "Twenty cents a week is a small price to pay for freedom." Of course, then there's human nature. Add another nickel and that makes it twenty-five cents, the same as a ticket to a movie.

Your friend,

Catherine

Pearl Harbor, Hawaii

MAY 11, 1941

Dear Catherine,

You were right. I should've confessed. Gordo came into my room a few days ago and said, "Boy, you're gonna get it now." Then he told me that Mother found out I went flying with Drew. One of the nurses from the Naval Hospital was at the airport that same day to ride in an airplane with her boyfriend, an Air Corps pilot, and saw me with Drew.

I felt horrible. I wish I could say I wasn't thinking, but I knew exactly what I was doing. I planned how to get to Honolulu early in the morning without anyone noticing anything out of the ordinary. I lied to my parents, to Helen and Drew. All so I could have a chance to fly.

It was the look on Dad's face that hurt the most. He said, "Your mother and I are deeply disappointed, Merrie."

I wish he'd called me Meredith.

"I'm so sorry," I whispered.

"Young lady," he snapped, "if you're old enough to fly without your parents' permission, you're old enough to sit up straight and look me in the eyes and speak up."

I did exactly that. "I know I disappointed you both. I wish I could say I wasn't thinking, but I wanted to fly so badly that I was willing to risk everything—even your trust in me."

"Which is more important to you?"

"Sitting here now, Dad, of course, I want you to trust me. But that day ... and the days leading up to it ... well, I couldn't get the idea of going up in that plane out of my mind. I thought about it until I had to know what it was like. I had to fly. I was willing to sacrifice it all to just have one part of my dream."

Dad said, "And you were banking on us not finding out?" I nodded.

Mother added, "We weren't saying no forever, just for now. But what you did shows us even more that you're not ready. You're not

responsible enough or mature enough to fly an airplane. You've violated our trust."

I knew in my heart they were right. My insides felt all torn open. At that moment, I wanted nothing more than to restore their trust in me. I had gambled and lost, but the payout wasn't worth it anymore. Now my memory of my first flight is filled with pain and lies and broken trust. Actually, it already was from the moment I first said yes to Drew. It's just that I kept pushing down the warnings I know the Lord was trying to give me. I had to have what I wanted right then and there.

"I want you to trust me again," I told my parents. "I'm sorry. I know it was wrong. Please forgive me. I understand if you can't, though. I did a horrible thing."

Dad answered, "We'll forgive you. But as for getting our trust back? That's for you to earn. Now we've discussed your punishment. First, you're grounded. We mean that literally. No more flying. We don't want to hear another word from you about it. Second, you're grounded for two weeks. No dances. No tennis. No swimming. No movies. No shopping. Nothing but church with the family."

"Third," Mother said, picking up where Dad left off, "you'll begin taking lessons at the Red Cross in first aid and donating your time to the Red Cross. I've arranged it with the Honolulu chapter. I don't want to hear any complaints either. You need to learn how to think of others first, and not just what you want to do. This will be a start."

"Finally," Dad said, "you'll need to talk with Drew and his parents and ask their forgiveness for violating their trust. I've talked with Drew's father, and he thought you had our permission or he'd never have let Drew take you up in the plane. I'll take you over there tomorrow night to talk with them. You've also violated Helen's trust. You used her to help your scheme, and she didn't even know it. And Lieutenant Clark. The father of your best friend. Do we need to spell out what you have to do?"

"No, sir, I understand."

I knew exactly what he was talking about. They asked me to go to my room and think about what they'd said and what I intended to do about it. Mom said, "I love your free spirit. I do. God gave it to you for a reason. But our job as your parents is to help you train that spirit so that it's truly free. Free to be everything God intended you to be."

I nodded. It was a long night. And several long days. I had many apologies to make and much forgiveness to seek. First, I had to go back to my parents and confess that I had wrangled a job at Andrews Flying Service. I told them everything. How I'd gotten the job, what I'd been doing the last two months, how much flying time I'd saved up. Dad looked at Mother, sighed, and walked out of the room. Mother gave me a stern look and said, "Add them to your list."

I told Helen first at lunch the next day at school. Helen told me she thought we had a better friendship than that. She's found someone else to sit with at lunch for the past few days. Dad drove me over to the Army base to meet with Drew and his parents. Dad stood by silently while I explained to Drew and his parents what I'd done and told them I was sorry I'd lied to them. The whole time I was talking, Drew sat there in a chair with his arms folded and looked past me. I think he heard what I said, but as soon as I was done, he jumped up, walked over to my father, and apologized to my father! Never in a million years, he said, would he have taken me flying without their permission. He just took my word for it that it was okay. "I should have talked to you first, sir," Drew said as he looked my father straight in the eye. Dad thanked him and shook his hand. Drew's father shot me a look that made me feel like I was not worthy to be around his son. I guess, really, I'm not.

Only your father seemed like he truly forgave me, but that in a way, was worse. He said, "A spirit of adventure without the disciplines of responsibility and trust will ultimately land you in a lot of trouble. Just like it has this time. I forgive you, and I believe in you. I know you'll find a way to earn your parents' trust back again." I sure hope so.

Your weary, but repentant friend,

Merrie

Pearl Harbor, Hawaii

MAY 14, 1941

Dear Catherine,

Mother lifted my grounding for one day. She drove Gordo and me to the Queen's Hospital, where the Red Cross, the Territorial Medical Society, and Company A of the 11th Medical Regiment at Schofield held a two-hour medical preparedness show. Mother directed me to the Red Cross first aid training table to sign up for my course.

We had a hard time rounding up Gordo later to hear General Short. Gordo had volunteered to be a wounded child in a first aid demonstration. He played the part so well the nurses and doctors didn't want to let him go. People practiced carrying poor wounded Gordo on a stretcher, as he moaned and groaned.

General Short told us it was our patriotic duty to store food. Mother looked at me and smiled. Oh no, more Spam. He applauded the Oahu Sugar Company for its donation of a large piece of land to teach eighth graders how to grow food. He encouraged everyone to take the Red Cross first aid course. As I wandered around the exhibits, I had to wonder. Does the general really think we will be attacked? Out here in the middle of the Pacific Ocean, thousands of miles from anywhere?

I saw Frank and Helen. Mother would only let me talk to them for a minute because I was technically grounded. Helen whispered that Drew was going to come with them, but his father took him to Hickam Field to watch the Flying Fortresses, the B–17 bombers, fly in. I dutifully pretended to be interested in all this first aid stuff with my mother, but my mind was on those airplanes. How I would have loved to watch them fly in to Hickam too. With Drew. Yeah, in my dreams.

Your friend,

Merrie

Pearl Harbor, Hawaii

MAY 20, 1941

Dear Catherine,

Honolulu had another practice blackout tonight. It only lasted from 9:00 p.m. to 9:30 p.m. Dad let Gordo and me go with him to a lookout to see it. It's a very strange sight. First, all the streetlights blink, and then go out. Then the sirens sound and church bells ring. Our battery-powered radio, which we took with us, told everyone to "Outblack the last Blackout!" At 9:00 p.m., the radio announcer shouted, "BLACKOUT!" Immediately, all the citizens of Honolulu turned out their lights. Drivers pulled to the curb and switched off their lights. All electric and neon signs were turned off. All at the same time.

The U.S. Army Air Corps simulated an air attack on every island in the territory. The planes roared overhead as they pretended to attack and bomb the city. According to the radio announcer, the best defense of an air raid is complete darkness. As the planes streaked past us in the inky night, we all stood silent. Dad put his arms around us both. It was eerie.

Your friend,

Mettie

Washington, D.C.

MAY 23, 1941

Dear Merrie,

I got your letter today about your parents finding out you flew with Drew. I can tell from your letter, I don't need to say anything else. I'll be praying, though. Dr. Marshall always tells us young people at church that God loves to make all things new again.

He says that when we've failed, and confessed the failure to God, we know He forgives us. But that's not enough. Dr. Marshall says that unless we're changed, we'll just do these same kinds of things again. He said that when we deliberately choose to do what we know is wrong, then we have to ask God to do something about our will. So, what I copied down from Dr. Marshall's prayer for us is what I shall be praying for you:

Lord, I acknowledge my total dependence on you. Make me over into the person you want me to be, that I may yet find that destiny for which you did give me birth.

The Cadet Hop is tonight. Most of the kids are going. I wasn't invited. It's the biggest event of the year. I told Mom I didn't care, but you know what? I guess I do. It hurts to feel unwanted. The girls dress up, the boys bring them corsages, and this year especially, because of the citywide victory, it promises to be an all-out celebration. Margaret's going with Patrick O'Malley, one of the Cadets.

We went to Woodies after school last week to go shopping for Margaret's new outfit for the dance. Printed Hawaiian skirts, made out of rayon, are definitely the fashion now. I guess you'd be right in style if you were here. There were lots of Western High girls there picking out outfits for the dance. I made the excuse to Margaret that I had to save my money for the Hank Fund anyway. She and I both know that's just an excuse. I wish I'd been asked to the dance. It seems like everyone's going. Margaret told me as gently as she could on the way home that she heard that Robert's taking Linda to the dance. Margaret's a good friend. I'm glad I heard it from her.

After dinner, Mother made us iced tea and got out Monopoly. We played for an hour and then I went to my room to write Hank, Daddy, and you. Mother just checked in on me again tonight for the fourth time. I think she's worried about me.

Your friend,

Catherine

Washington, D.C.

Dear Merrie,

Today Mother got a call from the Warm Springs Foundation. "Hank's had a setback," she told me when I came home. He fell today while practicing a few steps and broke his right arm and broke both bones in his left leg. The doctors performed surgery on his leg, but it's in bad shape. His leg will be immobilized for at least three months. They said if there ever was a chance for Hank to walk, it's likely gone now. They're not sure he'll even walk again with crutches.

That's more than a setback. That's the end of the line. It's not fair. Hank's been through so much, and finally, it seemed like things were turning around for him. We should've been there for him. We should be there for him now. I hate this disease. I hate what it's done to Hank and to our family. I begged Mom for us to go down to Warm Springs—right away—but we don't have enough money. I can't stand not being able to do something—anything—for Hank. Mom says we just need to pray, but it doesn't seem like enough. I feel so helpless.

Your friend,

Catherine

Washington, D.C.

June 3, 1941

Dear Merrie,

Has Hank heard, I wonder, that Lou Gehrig died yesterday? Less than two years ago he gave his emotional farewell speech at Yankee Stadium. When I arrived at the *Chronicle* today, Mr. Ward was slumped over his desk. He loves baseball as much as, if not more than, Hank. "Coffee?" I asked. He shrugged his shoulders. Not sure whether that was a yes or no, I brought him a fresh cup anyway to cheer him up. He muttered his thanks, but kept doodling on his paper. I looked over his shoulder. 23 grand slams, 184 RBI's, four home runs in one game, drove in 500 runs in 3 years, 2,130 consecutive games, Number 4 jersey. He had scribbled Mr. Gehrig's stats all over the paper.

I pulled up a chair next to his desk. "Mr. Ward?"

"Yeah, kid," he said, "kind of a rough day for me."

"I know, my brother thinks the world of Mr. Gehrig. He's been his inspiration these last two years. My brother's got polio. He's in Warm Springs now. His legs were paralyzed, and he was beginning to take some steps again. He used to say, 'If the Iron Horse won't give up, then I won't let this iron lung beat me either.'"

Mr. Ward sat up straight and spun his chair out on its wheels. He grabbed a sharpened, unchewed pencil from Mr. Sanders' desk, straightened up his pad of paper, and began to write furiously. A couple of minutes later, he said, "Tell me more, kid."

For the next hour, I poured out my heart about Hank. I told Mr. Ward about when he was diagnosed, how I saw Daddy cry for the first time ever, how Mom curled up for days on the sofa and sobbed, and how they wouldn't let us in at first because they told us he was contagious. I told how Daddy kept swinging Hank's bat outside and hitting pop-ups he pitched to himself and how I'd never forget the sound of the crack of his bat — Hank's bat — as it split the air.

I told him about Hank's courage when they tightened his braces. I described the sounds of Hank talking to me, pacing himself to catch the breath the machine was creating for him. In answer to his questions, I told of the doctor's grim diagnosis and the look on his face as he told us there was not much hope that Hank would ever walk again. I described the daily trips to the ward in the hospital where I'd read Hank the sports page and the Bible, or had listened to a baseball game on the radio with him.

Mr. Ward looked at me steadily while I told him about my brother. Then he said, "Write it all down, kid." He got up and told me to sit in his chair. "Write the story of what it's like to love someone who's suffering from an unexpected onslaught of a disease that changes everything—for everyone."

I sat down in his chair and picked up a pencil from the pile on his desk. I chose the one that was the most chewed and the least sharpened. It was Mr. Ward's favorite pencil. Then I began to write.

Mr. Ward ran copy for me while the words poured out on the page along with the emotions that had been bottled up inside for over a year. I wrote and wrote until there was a red mark on my finger from holding the pencil so tight. I poured my heart out, and the story was told. I rolled the chair back, left the papers on the desk, and walked out the door. Miss Gladstone called out, "Have a good night, doll."

I walked for two more hours. So many voices were inside my head. Peace that no storm of life can take away. In thy presence, restore our faith, our hope, our joy. Offer him sacrifices of thanksgiving. Hank's had a setback.

When I got home, Mom met me at the door. "Lou Gehrig died."

"I know," is all I said and I went to my room and closed the door. We were both thinking of Hank.

Your friend,

Catherine

Washington, D.C.

Dear Merrie,

As I came in the door to the *Chronicle* this afternoon, Miss Gladstone, smacking her gum, greeted me with her usual, "Hello, doll." When I entered the newsroom, the reporters stopped typing. Mr. Conner whispered to Mr. Sanders. I saw Mr. Ward get up quickly from his desk and go down the hall. None of them would look at me.

"What's going on?" I asked Mr. Conner. He turned away. "Mr. Sanders?" He just picked up his coffee cup and walked away. "I'll get your coffee."

"I'll get it myself," he said.

Mr. Ward came back in the room, and I went up to his desk. "What's wrong? Am I going to be fired?" Mr. Ward just sat down at his desk, propped his elbows on the table, and put his hand over his eyes.

Mr. Conner said, "Come on. Don't let her hear it from someone else. Just tell her."

Mr. Ward rose from his chair slowly, and said, "Catherine, you want to know what's going on?" Mr. Ward had never called me Catherine before. It's always, "Hey, kid."

"Okay, I'll tell you." I leaned on the desk to steady myself. I need this job to earn money for Hank.

"No!" The booming voice of Mr. McGurdy settled in over the room. He walked up to me with a folded newspaper tucked under his arm. Whipping it out, he slapped it on the table. "I'll tell you what's going on." I was shaking at this point. He pointed to an article on the second page of the sports section. I couldn't look at the paper. My mind was racing with how I might have messed it up. Had I pasted it wrong for the composing room? Had I mixed up the copy?

"Go ahead, kid, take a look," said Mr. Ward gently. I looked at the

two-column article. The title was "Iron Horse Inspires Iron Lung Patient to Never Give Up." The byline said "by Catherine Clark."

The reporters stood up, clapped their hands, and cheered. "That's our gal." "Hey, kid, way to go!" "Ace reporter!" Mr. Ward stuck one of his finest chewed up pencils behind my ear. Mr. McGurdy shook my hand and said, "Keep it up, Clark. This summer you're going to be a cub reporter. You'll learn everything from the bottom up, ya hear? No favors. Ward here will teach you everything you need to know. Your beat? Human interest. Keep this stuff coming. It's golden."

The reporters came up and each congratulated me. Jean was there and said her uncle had let her in on the secret, so she'd come in especially just to watch, but stayed hidden. She's very proud of me. She said that she has yet to get a story written that meets with her uncle's approval. Miss Gladstone came in with fresh coffee and doughnuts for everyone. "I always knew you could do it, doll," she said as she hugged me tight. The smell of her more-than-generous perfume mixed with the smells of cigarette smoke and printer's ink. I took it all in. I never want to forget this day.

Mr. Ward told me that he read the story after I left in such a rush after writing it. When he saw the slant I was taking in the story, he got an idea. The story was about Hank and his love of baseball and how the sudden onset of polio had stolen his dream but not his courage, no matter what the odds. If he tied in Lou Gehrig's influence on my brother, it would make a perfect human interest story. It would demonstrate the impact this man had on kids who not only looked up to him to learn how to hit better or to excel at baseball, but also how to excel at the game of life which sometimes throws you a curve ball. He wrote an introduction and tied the theme in, but otherwise the article is all mine.

I practically floated home after work. I couldn't wait to show Mom today's issue. Mr. McGurdy sent me home with five copies. I sent one to Hank, one to Daddy, and I'm enclosing one for you and your family. Mom's taking hers to the White House tomorrow

to show all her friends at work. She hopes she can show "Mrs. R" someday, so she's going to keep it in her desk. I stayed up late writing to you and Daddy and Hank. I couldn't sleep anyway. What a day!

Your friend,

Catherine

Pearl Harbor, Hawaii

JUNE 18, 1941

Dear Catherine,

I love your article! I'm so proud of you! And a cub reporter now — WOW! Congratulations. You're making your dreams come true! All that hard work is paying off. I'm so happy for you.

My first aid classes have begun. My teacher is Dan Morinaga, a senior next year at McKinley High. Misery loves company, that's what I say, so I had to get some company for this course. A few days before the class began, I ran into Janet and talked her into taking the course with me. And Helen too, now that she's talking to me again. Gwendolyn flat turned me down. "I'm not taking any course taught by a boy at Tokyo High." I couldn't resist. I told her that he was good enough for the American Red Cross, but she just tossed her hair and said, "At this rate, soon it'll be called the Japanese Red Cross." I even roped Frank into it. I told him that only trained kids can help out if the city's attacked. Frank doesn't want to miss out on any action. Frank talked Drew into signing up, but Drew doesn't have much to say to me these days.

When our lesson began, Dan said that we'll learn about bullet wounds, burn wounds, and puncture wounds, as well as simple sprains, strains, and cuts. Get this. After each blackout, doctors find more people need first aid. They're bumping into furniture in the dark!

The first class was all about blood. We studied a chart that showed where the arteries lie close to the bone and then practiced applying pressure at those points to stop the bleeding. Oh yes, Dan gave us a tip. If the blood's coming out in spurts, it's coming from an artery, and if it's coming out steadily, then it's coming from a vein. Great. Just what I wanted to know.

Dan encouraged us to donate blood after class. The Preparedness Committee wants as much blood and plasma on hand as possible. We learned that plasma is very effective to treat shock and burns, the most likely injuries in an attack. Attack? There's that word again. There's so much talk about it now that I'm having nightmares about being bombed.

After the class, Helen wanted to take me to the new Sears store that opened while I was grounded. But first, the kids (minus Drew who decided to donate some of his all-American blood) went to the Coconut Shack for lunch. We talked about the gruesome things we were going to learn to do, like how to apply tourniquets to torn-up arms and legs. Ugh. Our teacher is really good. He's seventeen, but he's been teaching first aid for a while now, ever since the preparedness classes got under way here.

Janet told us about a big rally of over 2,000 Japanese Americans held at McKinley High School a few days ago. The theme of the night was "Loyalty to the Nation and to the Government and to a Way of Life." She said it was a very moving demonstration of patriotism to America, and that everyone there pledged their loyalty to the United States. I looked at Helen. She didn't seem convinced.

I asked Janet if all this talk about being prepared for a Japanese attack makes her feel strange. She replied, "No stranger than it makes you feel. I'm American too."

Your friend,

Mettie

Washington, D.C.

JULY 6, 1941

Dear Merrie,

Enclosed is a clipping from Mrs. Roosevelt's newspaper column, "My Day," in the *Daily News* two days ago. It says, "Miss Jacqueline Cochran is lunching with us today, and I am most anxious to hear the report of her trip, about which I shall tell you more in a future column." When I asked Mom, she said that President and Mrs. Roosevelt did indeed meet with Miss Cochran at Hyde Park. She'd just returned from ferrying a Lockheed bomber to England. She was the pilot!

Miss Cochran told them fifty women pilots in the Air Transport Auxiliary in Britain ferry planes for the military there. Miss Cochran wants to start something like that here, but needs help getting her proposal to the right people in Washington. She left with a note of introduction from the president to the assistant secretary of war for air.

Can you believe the government won't let any more girls into the Civilian Pilot Training Program? They say every spot is needed for boys now.

It poured rain today. Mom and I had planned to go on a picnic and watch the fireworks at the Washington Monument tonight, but the ground was soaking wet. Instead, we stayed home, drank lemonade, and played Monopoly.

This weekend, we listened to the Yankees game. It made us both feel close to Hank, who we're sure was listening too. The unbroken Joe Dimaggio hitting streak of 45 games promised to make the game exciting enough. Add the unveiling of the Lou Gehrig memorial, and it was a "can't miss" game, as Hank says. When the Yankees won, it was even sweeter. Mom and I laughed till we cried, thinking of Warm Springs getting a hefty dose of Hank's enthusiasm. Oh, Merrie, how much I miss him!

Your friend,

Catherine

Pearl Harbor, Hawaii

JULY 7, 1941

Dear Catherine,

Dan told us that when the Preparedness Committee got started, there wasn't one good pair of surgical bandage scissors in all of Honolulu! They should've checked with Mother. She takes great pride in her surgical scissors.

I barely made it through the part of the class about surgical dressings. Dan, who wants to go to medical school, spoke very clinically about the need to use gauze rather than cotton cloth for a dressing because absorbent cotton sticks to a burn or wound. Ick.

Dan told us that any material can be used to hold a dressing in place, to keep a splint in place, as a sling, or to control bleeding by pressure. He demonstrated by taking off his tie and borrowing my scarf and tying the two together with a special knot and then using it to create a sling.

After class, Frank wanted to donate blood, so Drew went with us to the Coconut Shack. He walked with Helen on the way over. Helen and Janet worked it out to make sure Drew had to sit next to me. He asked me how my summer was going, and I told him about the tennis tournament. I asked him about how he liked the first aid course. Not one word from either of us about flying. When Frank showed up, Drew spent the rest of the lunch talking to him. I don't think Drew's ever going to forgive me. Good grief. I'm not perfect, you know. And who does he think he is anyway? He doesn't have to punish me forever.

There've been a lot of editorials in the papers lately about everyone remembering that the Japanese Americans in Hawaii are not our enemy. *The Honolulu Advertiser* said, "Pigment has nothing to do with loyalty or patriotism. Such qualities are found in the heart, such as devotion to America by those who have grown up from the soil with a growing America, or by those who have chosen America as their land."

I suppose the papers are trying to convince the Gwendolyns of the world. But lately, I guess I understand the fear. There's been so much talk these last few months about getting ready here for a possible attack or invasion. You can feel the tension in the air even when no one talks about it. I don't think anyone expects the Germans to fly over the United States to get to us. It's the Japanese that are likely to attack here.

Once we learned how to make bandages, we had to learn how to use them. We pretended there'd been an attack and we had to help wounded citizens with broken arms and legs. No cuts. No burns. Amazing. I guess the attackers were being nice today.

We took turns as the injured and the first aid worker. Drew had to suffer through my putting a sling on his arm. It took three tries to get the knot right so his forearm would be level. Then we had to try it with pins. I stuck him in the shoulder (accidentally, I promise!). Drew said, "Hey, Dan, over here. I think I'm being attacked again!"

Your friend,

Merrie

Pearl Harbor, Hawaii

JULY 16, 1941

Dear Catherine,

When you told me the government cut out the college training program for women fliers, my heart sank. When my parents nixed flying lessons, I still hoped I could learn to fly in college. I know Mother thinks this is just a fad. I wonder what she'll think when I save all my money, even if it's money I make as a nurse, until I can afford to learn to fly! I'm not giving up on my dream.

We've had two more first aid lessons—all on bandages. I never knew there were so many kinds of bandages. No body part should feel left out—each gets its own special way of wrapping the bandage. There's even a nose bandage! It's been a lot to learn.

I had to admit it. Mother and Dad were right. This course does sober you. When you realize that injuries could be life-threatening, you pay attention. Once we were past the spurting blood part, I've not minded it at all. Taking the course with my friends has been good too because we've had to practice on each other. We tend to be a competitive group, so we egg each other on. Next week—splints!

While we were bandaging each other one day, Dan told us that the Hawaiian Pineapple Company is building a huge warehouse to provide space for millions of pounds of food, probably mostly canned goods. Drew said, "Oh, man, that's a lot of pineapples!" If my mother has anything to do with it, those shelves will be filled with Spam.

This week Honolulu Gas Company taught a class on shortcuts in cooking so that women would have more time for Red Cross projects. Over two thousand women came! I teased Mother tonight about her favorite shortcut to dinner. I said, "Every time you open a can of Spam, you're helping America."

She said, "Thanks, at 29 cents a tin, I needed a reason to keep buying it. Anyway, it's a canned good. I can stock up on it." Gordo groaned. He hates Spam.

Your friend,

Merrie

Washington, D.C.

JULY 26, 1941

Dear Merrie,

Everyone's talking about President Roosevelt's "get your head out of the sand" fireside chat. He warned us not to wait until the bombs actually drop in the streets of New York or San Francisco or Chicago. Well, Washington, D.C. finally seems to be waking up to the idea of self-defense. The *Breeze* staff volunteered to help with the registration of civilians. Robert and I shared a table at the school to sign up folks for medical work, sewing, first aid, newspaper work, and driving ambulances. We both signed up for newspaper work—a perfect fit.

We couldn't talk much because there were so many people who came to register. Robert told me he was impressed with my article on Hank. I told him Mr. McGurdy promoted me to cub reporter for the summer. Robert asked if I'd get out to Glen Echo any of these weekends to meet the Western kids there, but I said it cost too much. I explained how Mom and I need to fill up the Hank Fund jar as fast as possible, what with Hank's broken bones. "Besides," I confessed, "I can't dance. Not like you anyway. I've got two left feet."

"Well, if you were a boy, that might keep you out of the Army," he said, "but since you're a girl, it's high time you learned. Why don't you let me teach you? It's easier than it looks." I blushed, and thankfully a family of six came up to offer their services and kept me busy for a while.

Robert said he'd like to go to the Naval Academy, but if he doesn't get in, he'll enlist right after graduation. That's just ten months away. He heard a rumor that Western might be offering extra courses in the fall for some kids who want to graduate early in the February class.

I thought as a cub reporter I might get some more interesting stories. All the stories I work on have a "human interest" element, but I'm not so sure they provide any news. Mr. Ward says, "Sure they do, kid. Color and texture. Otherwise, no one would read the newspaper."

Well, my color and texture has been limited to interviewing local Boy Scouts on the aluminum pots-and-pans collection drive, and writing an article on reindeer when the United States Navy landed at Iceland for our defense. I provided loads of great

information on the people and history of Iceland, but Mr. McGurdy told me to write about the reindeer. He thinks they're unusual and people will like them.

One bit of good news: the paper pays me to go to the movies now because I might find one good enough to write about, and I need to keep up with the newsreels. That's twenty-five cents for each movie I can save for the Hank Fund.

I'm especially nice to the copy boy who runs the subscriptions this summer. It's been a really hot summer. I make sure I have a glass of iced tea waiting for him when he comes in dripping with sweat. I sure don't miss those days.

Your friend,

Catherine

Pearl Harbor, Hawaii

August 6, 1941

Dear Catherine,

The military kids feel the tension here, and we compare notes. We know when maneuvers are stepped up. We can tell how worried our parents are. Why do parents always talk in low voices around kids when stuff is happening? That's a sure giveaway it's something bad. We're all anxious and imagining the worst. All these first aid lessons seem so scary. Am I really going to need to know this stuff?

Mother said the Red Cross Motor Corps is on regular duties now. The Navy's loaned vehicles to them, and each woman has a list of assignments for "Attack Day." That's what everyone's calling it now. It's so unreal! The papers tell us not to worry, all is well, just err on the side of caution and be prepared. Prepared for what? Attack Day!

Dan tells us we have to know our first aid inside and out. "You never know when you might need it to help someone." So he drills and drills us. We've gotten very proficient in our bandaging. Dan spent a lot of time on puncture wounds, the type that could be caused by bullets.

This week we learned to apply pressure to stop severe bleeding using just our hands. I can't imagine ever making myself do that! If the bleeding is severe and a compress is not around, we're to use the palm of our hand or fingers to stop the bleeding. He said, "It's better to have a live patient with a dirty wound than a dead patient with a clean wound." When would you have to work so fast you couldn't find some kind of bandage for pressure?

The girls finally decided to donate blood today. Maybe it was all the talk about blood spurting from arteries and flowing from veins. Double ick. As we rested on cots and let the blood drip out of our veins, we talked about the chances of an attack on Honolulu, what kind of wounds and injuries there might be, and what we'd like to do in a first aid station. Helen says it scares her, and she doesn't want to think about it. I agreed, but said it's easy to worry when all we learn in our classes is how to stop bleeding from wounds. It's how the wounds get there in the first place that gives me the willies. Janet was quiet. She changed the subject to ask me if things were warming up with Drew. Sure, I told her, about as warm as the North Pole.

When we met the boys afterwards at the Coconut Shack, they told us they're proud of us for finally doing our American duty and donating lifeblood to the wounded and injured. We all laughed, but it was good to see some respect for me in Drew's eyes.

At home that night, I told Mother she was right—learning to be prepared for emergencies has taught me more about thinking ahead. I never realized so much went into basic first aid training. I guess Gordo and I have been lucky with only some skinned knees. You, good friend, know how fragile life and health are. I've taken it for granted. But no more.

Your friend,

Merrie

Washington, D.C.

Dear Merrie,

Now what do you think was the exciting assignment I had this week? Get ready. It's a doozy. Women's reaction to no more silk stockings. All silk is needed now for parachutes. Mr. McGurdy sent me downtown to Woodies to get the scoop.

The morning after the government announced its embargo on silk from Japan, women lined up for blocks at the department store. Some women fear that without the silk, they'll have to paint their legs like the British women do. Another woman said she didn't believe nylon stockings will make a good substitute, and she's suspicious of these artificial fibers. The ladies at the back of the line, which was growing longer every minute, tried to act like they didn't care if the stockings were all sold out by the time they got in the store. They told me they have great hopes for the new stockings made out of cotton that is supposed to be very sheer.

The highlight of my investigation into this story was to witness the crowd reaction when the Woodies manager came out and announced each woman would be limited to two pairs only for purchase. The groans of these women must have been heard round the world!

Back at the paper, I tried to give my notes to Mr. Ward. He said, "Oh, no, kid. This one's all yours." So I sat down at my desk and wrote the article, "Embargo on Silk — Washington Women Snag Stockings." See? I am a fashion reporter, after all! Mr. McGurdy let me have a byline with Mr. Ward on this article, but I put it at the back of my scrapbook.

After I finished, and yelled, "Copy!" (which, by the way, is a tremendous thrill), I walked over to Georgetown Hospital to research a lead Jean gave me about new techniques to help polio patients. The medical librarian showed me several articles written about the Sister Kenny method. "Sister" is the medical officer title she got in the Australian military.

I pored over every detail of the treatment. Sister Kenny uses hot packs to relax the muscles. Then she retrains the muscles through massage and exercises to help them remember they are muscles. She's had tremendous success helping polio patients walk again—even when others have given up on them. I read all afternoon until it was time to go home. I took careful notes and kept a separate piece of paper with the questions I needed to follow up. The entire time I researched this, I thought of Hank. Maybe he can walk again!

I realize now why Jean gave me this lead. This summer we often walked down to the White House lawn to eat our lunch. I had told her how discouraged Hank was after he broke his leg and his arm. The doctors weren't sure whether to even let Hank try to walk again.

Sister Kenny says that muscles, which seem to be paralyzed, can be reeducated through careful muscle training. She urges doctors to stop splinting and immobilization. That's all that Hank's had—first in the iron lung, then in braces, and now this summer in a cast. Sister Kenny argues that all this does is make the muscles useless.

I rushed home and told Mom everything I'd learned. I shared my theory about why Hank's done so well in Warm Springs. Before he got hurt, he was at the pool every day. He doesn't just float around. He uses his arms to strengthen them for his crutches, and he moves his legs to make them "walk" in the water, which they can't do on the ground. He's using the warm water like Sister Kenny's hot packs, and the exercises like her therapy. The only problem is that when he leaves the pool, they put him right back in those braces.

I'm honestly starting to get my hopes up. Maybe this is the answer! We counted out the money in the Hank Fund. It's up to $44.77 now. Mom said, "I think we've got almost enough for two train tickets to Warm Springs. Perhaps by Christmas!"

I stayed up late to write to you tonight. I was much too excited to sleep. Now this is the kind of "human interest" story I want to write.

Your friend,

Catherine

Pearl Harbor, Hawaii

AUGUST 20, 1941

Dear Catherine,

East coast women gather in emergency rations of silk stockings, while here we prepare for Attack Day with food, medical supplies, bandages, air raid shelters, and evacuation plans. Our firemen train to put out incendiary bombs while your police make sure women don't mob the stores. What a weird world.

Speaking of preparedness, the past two weeks I've spent most of my time studying for my first aid exams. We talked about wounds, compresses, and anatomy at the dinner table. I practiced on Gordo. He definitely looked like a casualty of war!

When we arrived at the Red Cross training center for our exams, all of us, even Drew, were nervous. We took the two-hour written test first. Then Dan examined us on our first aid technique.

At the lunch break, we went to the Coconut Shack as usual, but we were on pins and needles. Frank wondered if he'd passed the written part. Drew said he couldn't remember the difference between a strain and a sprain. Janet and Helen said they know they mixed up the parts of the skeleton. I knew I had wrong answers too. I realized I wanted to pass—and pass with a high grade—much more than I thought I did.

After lunch, Dan said that there are two scores on the paper, one for knowing it right and one for doing it right. Our final score's an average of these two. I took my paper, held my breath, and looked: 92 percent written, 98 percent practical, average 95 percent Pass Plus. I was thrilled. Frank, Drew, Janet, and Helen all passed as well. Isn't that great?

We celebrated at Waikiki Beach with volleyball and swimming for the rest of the day. I left to go inside the Royal Hawaiian Hotel and find a telephone. This was one piece of news I didn't want to wait until I got home.

Drew asked me if I wanted to go for a walk. We walked along the beach without saying much for a while. Then Drew said, "You've changed this summer. You seem more serious."

"Is that a bad thing?"

"No," Drew responded, "I like it. I have to admit, I was really angry at you this spring."

"Oh, I certainly got that message."

"The truth is, I guess I'm kicking myself for not asking your parents' permission to take you flying in the first place. It was easier to blame you than take responsibility myself."

"I guess we both learned something this summer." Then I added, "Is it okay to talk about flying again? You haven't mentioned it once this summer."

"I guess I figured if I didn't bring it up, we could both just forget it. Sure, we can talk about flying."

"Does this mean you finally forgive me? I've had my apology hanging out there for three months now!" Drew shrugged his shoulders sheepishly and nodded. I took that for a yes.

We talked nonstop for the next hour. At least we're talking again, Catherine—about flying!

Your friend,

Mettie

Washington, D.C.

Dear Merrie,

Now that I'm a junior, I don't feel like a stranger at Western High anymore. When I got there this morning, the fashion girls were huddled in their usual group, ignoring everyone else but the boys. It still hurts that they ignore me, but I said a cheery hello to them as I walked past.

I headed up to the *Breeze* office to pick up any assignments. Robert asked me to cover the fall fashions since I did a good job on the silk stockings article. I groaned and said, "Oh yes, please. I love to write articles like this." Picking up the latest issue of the *Breeze*, I read: "The school girls' dream is the flannel blazer, and it comes in all sorts of luscious shades." Robert laughed and asked me if I would rather cover the flag salute story or the Junior Red Cross. Two good choices, but I took the flag salute story. I remembered the interview last year with the two boys from England who were puzzled by the way we saluted the flag.

I'll work two afternoons a week at the *Chronicle* now that school has started. On my last full day there, Mr. McGurdy said, "Well, Clark, we're gonna have to get by without you, but I don't know what I'm gonna do if there's a fashion crisis in this city again." I don't think I'll ever live down that story. Mr. Ward told me they'll have to give up my desk to another reporter, but I can always pull up a chair to work at his desk. I stood there for a minute surveying the chewed pencils, the four coffee cups, and the crumpled paper covering the desk, and started to laugh. "Okay, but make sure I only write the one-inch columns!"

I've got great teachers and yes, I'm still in the History Club. Classes are over at 1:30 p.m. this year, so I'll have more time to work on articles for the *Chronicle* and the *Breeze*, and to do my research on Sister Kenny's methods.

I noticed the girls aren't buying the latest jewelry anymore. No more strings of pearls. This year, everyone's wearing necklaces made out of dried macaroni with beads strung on a long ribbon. Extra money goes to buy defense bonds instead.

I wish I could be there to celebrate your birthday with you. I'm sending your present early to make sure it gets there in time. It's a necklace I made for you out of macaroni and beads. Now you can be just as fashionable as the next Western High girl.

Okay, that's definitely enough fashion from me in one letter!

Your friend,

Catherine

Pearl Harbor, Hawaii

OCTOBER 1, 1941

Dear Catherine,

School's great this year—especially now that Drew and I are talking again. I'm keeping busy playing a lot of tennis. There's been less talk about Attack Day, but I still feel it. It's like we're on pins and needles, waiting, and at the same time, trying to forget that it could happen.

I haven't seen much of Janet lately. Her father insists she stay close to home. I invited her to our weekly Bible class at the Honolulu Bible Training School. Mr. Downing, our teacher from the *West Virginia*, just got married to a swell gal. She wants to start a Bible study with just the girls. I invited Helen too, but she told me that if Janet comes, she won't join, which really irritates me. First Gwendolyn, and now Helen. Is the whole island so scared of the Japanese that we can't even be in a Bible study together?

Your friend,

Mettie

Pearl Harbor, Hawaii

OCTOBER 25, 1941

Dear Catherine,

You're not going to believe what happened tonight! My parents threw me a surprise birthday party at the Royal Hawaiian Hotel! We danced for hours. All my friends were there, and your dad! Mother invited Drew's parents. I felt embarrassed around them at first as I thought back to the last time I was with them. But they acted like nothing was wrong, so I decided to act that way too.

The gang all left around eleven, except your father, plus Drew and his family. Dad said there was one more present for me. I couldn't imagine what it might be, but from the way Gordo was jumping from one foot to the other and peering at the door, I knew it had to be something good.

Suddenly, the doors to the room flew open and in burst Miss Guild and a friend of hers. "Are we too late for the party?" Miss Guild asked breathlessly.

"Come in!" Dad said. He motioned to the waiter, who passed around fruit drinks with little umbrellas in them. Then Dad turned to me. "You've wanted to fly for a long time, and we've all experienced some of your creative ways to achieve it." Well, that got a big laugh out of everyone. I felt sheepish with Drew's parents there. "We're proud of the way you met our challenge this summer. You didn't try to get out of it. You didn't complain."

Mother nodded. "We think you're ready for challenges of your own now." Dad gave me an envelope, and said, "As our birthday present to you, to celebrate your life and your dreams, and to see if this is part of God's plan for you, your mother and I give you ... twelve hours of flying lessons with Miss Cornelia Fort of Andrews Flying Service."

I felt as if I had taken off in the air at that very moment. I was stunned, exhilarated, thrilled, amazed, enthralled, excited, oh, I can't think of enough words to tell you how I felt. I threw my arms around

Mother and Dad, Miss Guild, Miss Fort, Drew, Drew's parents, your father, and Gordo. I even gave the waiter a hug, I was so excited.

After I calmed down a bit—just a bit—Miss Guild introduced her friend, Cornelia Fort, the newest flight instructor with Andrews Flying Service, who'll be my flight instructor. Miss Fort said it takes only eight hours of flying time to solo, but that she and my parents had agreed on twelve hours of lessons before my solo flight. Miss Fort also said that they'd agreed that if my studies suffered, then the flying lessons would be on hold until my grades came back up. "Agreed?" she asked.

"Agreed!" I shouted.

"Then it's my great privilege to give you this present from your friends at Andrews Flying Service," she said as she handed me a brightly wrapped box tied in red ribbons. I tore at the ribbons and lifted a pair of aviatrix goggles out of the box. Everyone got another round of hugs and kisses while Gordo tried on the goggles. He used the back of a chair and a dinner knife as a rudder and a stick to pretend to take off into the night air.

Miss Guild said that the trade winds are very tricky in Oahu for smaller planes in the afternoon. For beginning flyers, the best time to learn to fly is the early morning. My lessons will be Saturdays at 6:30 a.m. sharp at John Rodgers Airfield. Each lesson is forty-five minutes long. Dad says I must wear a parachute for all my lessons. Just seven more days until my first lesson! Mom thinks it'll take that long for me to be calm enough for her to trust me in a cockpit.

Catherine, Catherine, Catherine, can you believe this? My greatest wish in all the world came true tonight!

I could not be happier in all the world! Oh, dear friend, yes, I could—if you were here to share this. I know, someday, I'll take you up with me in the plane. Together we'll soar above the earth and touch the skies. As close to heaven as one can get this side of eternity.

And at least for one night, we all forgot about preparing for Attack Day.

Your friend,

Merrie

Washington, D.C.

OCTOBER 31, 1941

Dear Merrie,

I went on a hayride in Rock Creek Park with a bunch of kids from the *Breeze* staff. Robert was there, and so was Linda, but they weren't there together. We laughed at the horses who snorted as they pulled the wagon because it seemed like they were singing along with Bill and his guitar. Afterwards, we had a bonfire and cocoa and hot cider.

National defense in America and at Western is the theme of the History Club this year. I do love the History Club. I know, I know. You want me to get out there and learn to dance and to have more fun. But I really am having fun now.

Here's a copy of the article I wrote on the flag salute. We had a school assembly to teach everyone the new salute. We used to salute the flag by raising our right hand straight out toward the flag, no bend at the elbow. Well, that certainly won't do anymore. We'd look too much like Nazis! No wonder our English refugees were surprised about our flag salute. The new one's the same one our armed forces use.

I interviewed Ken Erskine, who graduated from Western five years ago, for an article for the *Breeze*. He took flight lessons while he was a sophomore at Western and soloed when he was only fifteen! He's now the pilot of the Yankee Clipper.

All eight senior high schools offer the aviation course this year. Mr. Erskine said that learning to fly is an important part of America's future. I'm sure Mr. Erskine was thinking of boys, but why shouldn't a girl learn to fly? Golly, Merrie, if all the boys go off to war, who's going to fly those Yankee Clippers, anyway?

Your friend,

Catherine

Pearl Harbor, Hawaii

NOVEMBER 1, 1941

Dear Catherine,

I was up at 5:00 a.m., dressed and ready to go. After a wonderful breakfast Mother cooked for us that I couldn't eat a bite of, she put a beautifully wrapped gift on the table in front of me with a note: "Fly High! Love, Granddaddy." I tore open the wrapping, and inside was a leather helmet that fit perfectly.

Gordo teased me all through breakfast that he's going to bring his walkie-talkies to call the medics and his camera to record the crash landing. Mother told Gordo to stop three times. Dad had asked me if I wanted Drew to come with us to watch me have my first lesson, but I nixed the idea. I was nervous enough as it was. What if, after all this, I'm no good at flying?

We arrived at the airstrip twenty minutes early. Miss Fort taught another lesson before mine. I watched her plane land and taxi to a stop. She jumped down and greeted my parents and Gordo, who was busy snapping pictures. Then she turned to me. "Ready, Miss Lyons?" I swallowed hard. This was it.

We spent over half the lesson doing a preflight check. Miss Fort carefully explained everything about the Piper Cub. I tried to concentrate on all she said, but my thoughts were racing. Part of me repeated everything she said; part thought about what it would be like when we were up in the sky. I had to shush that part so I could hear Miss Fort's instructions.

She ran through the list of what every pilot must do for their preflight takeoff check to make sure the plane is safe to fly. We checked the fuel to make sure there was no water in it. We checked the engine and tubes and ports to see if they were stopped up. We checked the tires and belting on the wheels. We looked at the fabric on the wings to see if there were any breaks. Of course there weren't. I'd globbed the goop on this plane myself. I tried to feel like a flight student, but it seemed so unreal. It might as well just have been me in my coveralls with my pot of hot goop, checking for tears on the wings. Then we ran our fingers along the wooden propeller to find any gouges or nicks. We climbed up to check the celluloid windshield for any oil slicks that might show a problem with the engine.

After this, we climbed up into the cockpit. The trainer has two seats, one in front of the other. Miss Fort was in the front, and I was in the back. They both have rudder pedals and sticks and throttles. She told me that she was going to take the plane up in the air, and I was to keep my feet on the pedals and my hand on the stick and just feel what she was doing. Her pedals would control my pedals, and her stick would control my stick. My job was to just feel what the plane was doing while she did a simple run. "Are you ready?" she asked again.

"Ready!" I tucked my hair under my helmet and tightened my goggles.

She started the engine, and I felt the plane vibrate to life. She taxied the Piper Cub down the gravel runway. I placed my feet gently over the rudder pedals and held the stick in my right hand. Soon we were climbing into the air. We only climbed today to about 1,000 feet. Miss Fort told me later she just made a short run, flying back behind where we took off. She followed a simple pattern and returned with the downwind leg to line up with the runway again, watching for the windsock to tell us how to land. It may have only been a few minutes in the air, but it was all I needed to know. I was born to fly!

I can't wait until next week! Will my feet ever touch the ground again?

Your friend,

Merrie

Pearl Harbor, Hawaii

November 7, 1941

Dear Catherine,

I learned today about the throttle and how the ailerons and the rudder work together for turns. It all sounded so easy in the classroom, but in the air it's confusing. So much to keep straight! Drew says it will come with practice. I sure hope so! There's left aileron pressure and left rudder and back pressure applied at the same time for a left turn. To roll out of the turn, you apply the right aileron and the right rudder at the same time as well as relax the back pressure out of the bank. It reminds me of riding a bike. I know that sounds crazy, but in some ways it's like working the hand brakes and the pedals and the balance all at once. Trouble is, I crashed a lot learning to ride my bike. I can't afford that now!

Miss Fort wants me to focus on what she calls the four fundamentals: (1) the turn, (2) the climb, (3) the descent, and (4) the straight and the level. She started the engine again and did the takeoff, but this time I watched and felt everything she did on the takeoff and climb. It's starting to feel more natural. A little, anyway.

When we leveled off, she yelled back to me that it was time for turns. She motioned to the left. I tried to remember everything she taught me, but there's so much! I prayed hard for help.

Look out left. "Clear left," I shouted. Left aileron pressure. Left rudder. Back pressure. All applied at the same time. Roll into the turn. Easy now. Bank in. Easy on the wheel. Nose up gentle. Now relax back pressure. Don't let the nose drop. Roll out now.

Miss Fort signaled okay and then pointed to the right. I tried another turn to the right this time, but came in a bit shallow. I was suddenly petrified, like I didn't have any control. I panicked and signaled for Miss Fort to take over. But she wouldn't! I had to get control, but I wasn't sure how. She kept directing me with hand signals until I was level again, then she took over and took the plane back for a landing.

I could hardly get out of the plane, I was shaking so much. I was terrified and angry at myself. I didn't want to be afraid — not of flying — but I was.

When we landed, she said I have a good sense of where the reference points are for the wingtips and the nose in line with where I am and that soon, I'll be able to smooth out the turns. We're going to try again next week, and then it's on to climbing. When my heart finally stopped pounding, I made a promise to myself. I haven't come this far to stop now. I'm going to practice in my imagination every night before going to bed. I'll relive those minutes in the sky, feeling those turns over and over again until I can get them right.

Your friend,

Mettie

Washington, D.C.

NOVEMBER 14, 1941

Dear Merrie,

I had dinner ready when Mom came home from work today. "I have some bad news," she said. "We're not going to Warm Springs at Christmas after all." I put the soup ladle down on the stove and stared at her. Then she rushed to me, put her arms around me, and said, "We're going to Warm Springs for Thanksgiving!"

"Mrs. R" came by Mom's desk today and said she understood we were planning to visit Hank at Christmas. Mom told her that if her calculations were right, she'd have enough money for two tickets to Warm Springs by the middle of December. "Mrs. R" wondered if Mom would like to ride on the Presidential Train to Warm Springs before then. Can you imagine? We'd ride with the reporters who travel with the president.

Mom and I linked arms and danced around the living room. I couldn't believe what I was hearing. The president plans to spend a week there. I can't believe it. The Presidential Train! With the president! This will be the scoop of a lifetime. Wait until Mr. McGurdy hears about this.

Your friend,

Catherine

Pearl Harbor, Hawaii

November 14, 1941

Dear Catherine,

Today I learned how to climb. I didn't feel ready. I wanted to stay on the turns for a while. I felt the panic rising. What if I can't do this, I thought. Miss Fort had already explained about what makes the airplane yaw to the left on takeoff and how to correct for torque. It was my turn to try now. I prayed, breathed deep, and eased the nose up and increased to climb power. The plane climbed in the air as the speed built. Miss Fort signaled me again, and I eased off the right rudder and adjusted the power, and we leveled off. An okay sign from Miss Fort made me prouder than anything. I felt so relieved, I was weak.

We practiced straight climbs, level turns, and then climbing turns. The forty-five-minute lesson was over in a flash. It seems like the fastest minutes in the world are the ones I spend in that Piper Cub every week.

I did Gordo a favor today. I took his Captain Midnight Secret Squadron Code-O-Graph with me in the Cub today. Gordo pretended my plane was the sleek aircraft of Captain Midnight, and I was the able crew member, Joyce. Well, at least in the radio show, Captain Midnight let her in as an official Squadron member. Her abilities to assist in the fight against evil and to help save the world didn't go unnoticed by her mentor. I guess it's only in fiction that women pilots can make a difference. Maybe someday.

Your friend,

Merrie

Washington, D.C.

Dear Merrie,

We were supposed to leave today, but it's now rescheduled for Monday afternoon. We'll probably only have a few hours' notice to meet at Union Station. It all depends on the president's schedule. Mom and I are packed and ready to go. I don't think either of us slept much this past week. We're counting the minutes until we see Hank.

As I predicted, Mr. McGurdy is ecstatic. He even called me Catherine once. Mr. Ward gave me lots of tips for interview questions if I get the chance, six of his very best pencils (not one of them is chewed), and three reporter's pads of paper. I told him that the only people I might be able to interview are the other reporters who'll interview the president. He said he knew I'd find a way to make a story out of the trip somehow.

I have another story idea that I'd like you to think about. I'd like to run a series of your letters in the *Breeze* about learning to fly. I kicked the idea around with Robert today, and he likes it a lot. With the emphasis on getting high school students (the boys, at least) interested in aeronautics, he thinks these letters would be just the thing. He said you're a good writer, very descriptive, and he'd like to edit the letters lightly and print them as a column in the *Breeze* for the next two issues. Would you like that?

I'm so proud of you. You're a natural-born aviatrix!

Your friend,

Catherine

Aboard the Presidential Train

NOVEMBER 28, 1941

Dear Merrie,

After two postponements, we got word that this was it. We're finally leaving for Georgia. We rushed to Union Station. Mom learned Warm Springs Foundation postponed their Thanksgiving Dinner until Saturday. We won't miss celebrating with Hank after all.

We left Union Station on the Southern Crescent to Atlanta, where we changed trains to Newnan. I learned from the reporters why the president couldn't leave on time. Special Ambassador Kurusu arrived from Japan to meet Ambassador Nomura to discuss peace with the United States.

Saturday night, November 29th at Warm Springs, Georgia

The train swayed from side to side all night as it made its way south. Neither Mom nor I got much sleep though. We arrived in Newnan on Saturday morning. Basil O'Connor, the president of the National Foundation of Infantile Paralysis, greeted President Roosevelt. The two of them, along with Miss Tully, the president's secretary, rode to Warm Springs together. The president, in his deep blue Navy cape, looked very much like the commander in chief.

We'd hardly gotten settled in when there was a knock on the door. A member of the president's staff said Mr. Roosevelt might have to return to Washington immediately. They'd ordered the train back from Atlanta to be ready at a moment's notice. Mom asked if we had to return on the Presidential Train, and was told no.

Mom told me she'd brought our Hank Fund money just in case. If we needed to, we could buy one-way tickets home. I was terribly torn. The reporter in me wanted to go with the president. There surely must be some serious reason if he has to return quickly. The sister in me wanted to stay here with Hank. As soon as we saw

Hank, however, the decision was instantly made. If an immediate return is required, I'll stay here.

We found Hank glued to the radio and cheering on the Navy in the Army-Navy football game. He's out of his casts, but the doctors are still concerned about his leg. They didn't give us much hope that Hank will be able to do much more than stand and take a few steps. Walking again, they said, was out of the question. Hank sat in his wheelchair, legs bound up in those metal braces. His crutches stood by his bed. I knew instantly what Mom and I were thinking—hot packs and muscle massage and stretching. If only they'd adopt Sister Kenny's method here at Warm Springs! I'm no longer so sure Hank couldn't walk again.

I brought Hank a packet of my articles and as many sports clippings as I could stuff into the large manilla envelope. Mr. Ward sent Hank a Joe DiMaggio baseball card. Mom brought him his Yankees baseball cap and letters from Dad to read. Late in the afternoon, Mom and I returned to our cottage to dress for Thanksgiving Dinner. After all, we were dining with the president!

After a service in the chapel, we went to Georgia Hall for the dinner. The president sat at the head of a long table with the children all around him. He has a great laugh and loves to joke with them. After the meal, the patients performed a skit that made him laugh even more.

The president gave a short speech. Mom took notes in shorthand for me, so I could quote his remarks for my article. Mr. Roosevelt talked about the weekend football games he had listened to on the radio that day and asked, "How many other countries in the world have things like that going on?" He reminded us of how long the peace has been for America, but warned that it may not continue. "It may be that next Thanksgiving these boys of the Military Academy and Naval Academy will be actually fighting for the defense of these American institutions of ours."

The president, true to his tradition, was at the door to say good night to each of us and to shake our hands. I was not a reporter then.

I was just a girl who couldn't believe I was shaking the hand of the president of the United States.

It was his words to Hank that I'll never forget. "I've heard about you, Hank," he said. "Mrs. Roosevelt has kept me informed about your progress here. Never give up, Hank. Victory is sure." I wasn't sure whether the president was speaking about Hank's illness or the free world. I suppose both Hank and the nations of the free world are battle-weary. I suppose both of them need to be reminded that defeat is not an option.

We stayed in the lobby of Georgia Hall to watch the president say good-bye to others. I wanted to soak in all the details of this scene for my article and hear what he said to each person. It wasn't long, however, before one of the Secret Service men came to get the president to take a telephone call at his cottage. He left quickly, and Mom and I wheeled Hank back to his ward.

I wondered if that call was about the peace talks. If there's no hope for peace with Japan, then there's likely going to be a war somewhere in the Pacific. Thoughts of Daddy filled my mind, as I'm sure it did Mom's too. Give Daddy an extra hug and kiss for me the next time you see him. Tell him I love him.

Your friend,

Catherine

Pearl Harbor, Hawaii

NOVEMBER 30, 1941

Dear Catherine,

Wasn't the Army-Navy game incredible? I'm sure you listened to it. When Army was leading at the end of the first half, I was worried. We pulled it out though. Better luck next year, Army! Your father listened to the game with us, but he was on duty for Thanksgiving. We warmed up some leftovers for him.

As we drove to church, Dad said it doesn't look good here for any kind of peace with Japan. The Army and Navy made a decision to move all the aircraft carriers and half of the Army planes from the Pearl Harbor area. They expect Japan to make its move soon. Dad thinks maybe in the Philippines. He's had to go to more meetings about medical triage and plans for the Naval Hospital. He's quieter than normal, and he hasn't taken Mother out dancing in a long time.

At church, everyone talked about the headlines in today's *Honolulu Advertiser*: "JAPANESE MAY STRIKE OVER WEEKEND. KURUSU SAYS THAT HIS NATION IS READY FOR BATTLE." The Army's supposed to patrol all electrical, water, and communications plants to make sure they aren't sabotaged.

Early evening, the hospital called all nurses in for an unscheduled drill. Mother tossed her supplies in her nurse's bag and began to open cans. She opened a can of Spam, a can of pineapples, and bottles of Coca-Cola. Trying to avoid another night of Spam, I suggested Mother leave it in our storeroom as part of our "readiness supplies." Mother seemed to be thinking of other things as she mixed the Spam with the pineapple and plopped globs of it on plates for Gordo and me. Dad's already on duty tonight. Gordo rolled his eyes, and I gave him an elbow.

We hugged Mother as she left, then scraped the plates into the

garbage. We made peanut butter sandwiches instead. Gordo asked why our parents are acting weird. I didn't want to frighten him, so I changed the subject.

Your friend,

Merrie

Warm Springs, Georgia

December 2, 1941

Dear Merrie,

Sure enough, Sunday morning, we heard the president was going back to Washington. At 1:00, the staff, many of the patients, Mom, Hank, and I lined the driveway to wave good-bye. The president, again in his blue Navy cape, waved in return, and shouted, "I'll see you in the spring if we don't have war."

Mom and I got to spend two more days here after that, but we leave this afternoon on the train. Miss Tully, the president's secretary, sent us two return tickets on the Southern Crescent, so we didn't have to use the Hank Fund after all. Mom told me she has new plans for the fund. She wants to buy bus tickets to Minnesota to visit Sister Kenny's clinic. What a great idea!

These last two days, we've spent every minute we could with Hank. Even though it was a bit nippy, he talked Emerson into taking him into the pool so he could show us his exercises. He said some of these exercises President Roosevelt designed himself. Mom and I huddled on the bleachers. I squeezed Mom's hand as Hank called out, "Now watch this. This helps my legs loosen up."

We spent time together as a family in the chapel, praying for each other and praying for Daddy. Hank asked me to read from the Bible. He closed his eyes as I read from Psalm 23. Yea, though I walk through the valley of the shadow of death, I will fear no evil: for thou art with me.

It's so hard to leave Hank. Especially for Mom. I watch her sit next to him and read Daddy's letters to him one by one. I hear the ache in her voice for our family to be together again. Mom has been a good soldier, never once complaining. She's been apart from Daddy many times before; life in the Navy is like that. But never like this, with Hank so far away too. Oh, Merrie, when will we ever be together again?

Your friend,

Catherine

Pearl Harbor, Hawaii

DECEMBER 6, 1941

Dear Catherine,

We had to write a theme this week for English class: "How Football Promotes Unity." No kidding! I don't know how much unity the Navy had last weekend with the Army when we whooped them!

I invited Miss Fort to come to church with us tomorrow, but she's got an early-morning lesson to teach. When Dad came to pick me up after my last lesson, he said he's got another recruit for her, a young doctor who wants to do missionary aviation after he's out of the Navy. He told Miss Fort that a doctor who's also a pilot could bring supplies and medicines to the missionaries, and then be there on hand to help out.

"Creative idea," she said. "I like that. That's why I'm in aviation too, you know. It's not just to teach people to fly, though that's important." She looked my way. "Women pilots can make a difference too."

"How?" I asked. "By teaching men to fly?"

"That too, but my dream is bigger. Women can be an important factor in the national defense program. Women can do in this country what they've been doing in England—ferrying planes from factories to airports, flying the mail, and doing transport work for the government. Every woman who flies releases a man to fight."

"If anyone gets a shot at that, I bet it'll be you," said Dad.

I said, "My friend's mother works for Mrs. Roosevelt. She said Jackie Cochran's trying to convince the president to do just that, have women aviators ferry planes for the military."

Miss Fort laughed and said, "Well, then, perhaps we'll finally get to see what the women aviatrixes of America can do. Until then, Miss Lyons, study hard, and I'll see you next Saturday."

Ask your mother what's happening with that program. Miss Fort would be perfect for it. And me too, one day! I just need to solo first.

Your eyes on the sky friend,

Merrie

Pearl Harbor, Hawaii

DECEMBER 6, 1941, LATE AT NIGHT

Dear Catherine,

Two letters in one day! I just couldn't rest until I wrote to you about the fun we had today after my lesson.

Dad and your father had tickets to the University of Hawaii football game. At the last minute, your father had a patrol plane engine that needed attention, and then Dad got paged for an emergency operation. Dad suggested I call Drew to see if he wanted to go to the game. He wrangled another ticket so Gordo could come too. The Rainbows whipped Willamette 20 to 6.

After we dropped Gordo off at home, Drew and I went to Bloch Arena to the Battle of Music. Ever since they started this competition, it seems to get better and better. These boys really try to outdo each other. Tonight the bands from the USS *Pennsylvania*, the USS *Tennessee*, and the USS *Argonne* competed. The jitterbug contest got the place hopping. I can't wait for the final competition. I still think the USS *Arizona* band can't be beat.

Mother just came in and told me to turn out the light and the radio. We've been listening to KGMB all day when we were in the car. Everyone's relieved with the news in the paper today that the Japanese have offered another peace plan. Drew told me KGMB will be playing music all night to act as a radio signal for the Flying Fortresses that are coming in from California to Hickam Field.

Mother leaves at 5:30 a.m. tomorrow for nursing duty, and Dad's on call all night tonight at the hospital. I'm to fix Gordo breakfast in the morning and get him over to the MacAlistairs by seven o'clock so they can take him with them to church. He's going rock climbing with Jeff and his brothers after church.

I'll have time out on the patio with my Bible and a glass of juice before it's time to go to church myself. I love these quiet mornings

here in Hawaii. This place is so full of beauty, but never like I see it from the air with the sugarcane fields spread out below and the clear blue skies with the sparkling waters shining like crystal. Creation is a glorious thing. And I suppose if I'm going to enjoy God's creation tomorrow, I best enjoy God's sleep tonight.

I read a really great psalm today, Psalm 32:

> Thou art my hiding place; thou shalt preserve me
> from trouble; thou shalt compass me about with songs of
> deliverance. I will instruct thee and teach thee in the
> way that thou shalt go; I will guide thee with mine eye.

Good night, dear friend. I'll write again soon.

Your friend,

Mettie

Washington, D.C.

DECEMBER 6, 1941

Dear Merrie,

I wrote my article about Thanksgiving at Warm Springs on the way back in the train and took it to Mr. Ward at the *Chronicle* as soon as I returned. He read it, made edits, and turned it in to Mr. McGurdy, who said only, "Clark, you're coming along." I took this as a compliment.

Mr. Ward told me that the president had cut his visit short after Japanese Premier Tojo issued a statement threatening to "purge with a vengeance" all U.S. and British influence in the Far East. Mr. Ward thinks the Japanese will likely attack us in the Pacific soon, possibly the Philippines.

I also wrote an article on the train for the *Breeze* about the president's visit to Warm Springs. I wrote a second article about the Sister Kenny method compared to what I saw used in Warm Springs. Robert told me he'd think about including the second article, but that it was likely the *Breeze* would print only the first one. You know, "human interest." Robert says the "I was there" type articles are particularly readable.

The past few nights I've found myself going through Hank's collection of baseball cards and sorting them by team, then by season, then by position of the players, and then re-sorting them all again. Mom sorted and re-sorted his clothes. He only took a few things with him when he went to Warm Springs. I think we're trying to be as close to Hank as we can.

We got two letters from Daddy while we were gone. He's pleased with the Navy's patrol planes and says Kaneohe has a strong base there. He sent us the next verse to memorize. It's the same one he sent to Hank: Psalm 57, verse 1:

Be merciful unto me, O God. Be merciful unto me: for my soul trusteth in thee: yea, in the shadow of thy wings will I make my refuge, until these calamities be overpast.

Mr. Ward invited me to go to the Redskins football game tomorrow with him and his son. He wants to teach me how to cover sports news. I know it's Sunday, but Mom gave special permission for me to go. Wait until Hank hears about this!

Your friend,

Catherine

Pearl Harbor, Hawaii

DECEMBER 8, 1941

Dear Catherine,

It was horrible! The most terrifying day of my life. I'll never forget it. Never. I'm still scared. Shaking. I don't think you'll even get this letter, but I have to write it down. Maybe then it won't seem so horrid. I'm sure you're frightened too, wondering about your father. I wish I'd seen him yesterday, but then again, with what I was doing, and the horrors I saw, it's probably good I didn't.

About 8:00 a.m., I heard the droning of airplane engines. I didn't think much of it at first. Our Navy pilots are often on maneuvers. An explosion ripped through the air. Then another. I raced outside. I saw the blazing fires and smoke. I realized this was no practice drill. The smoke was black, not white like in practice drills. More planes flew over. I saw the bright red sun symbol on the wings. The Japanese were bombing the ships at Ford Island! People ran out of their homes in pajamas or church clothes. We all looked at each other in disbelief, terrified. *Attack Day* was here.

I could see the Naval Hospital from where I stood. More airplanes flew overhead. A Japanese plane that looked like it was burning flew straight at the front of the main hospital building. "Mother!" I screamed and ran to get a better view. The plane swerved to the left, struck the laboratory building, and crashed on our tennis court!

Women, some dressed, some in robes, rushed their children back into the house as shrapnel started to fall. Men in pajamas ran into the house and came back a minute later in uniform. I stared into the sky. Black clouds of dense smoke filled the air and mixed with the low-hanging clouds. Shrapnel rained down on us. I rushed back inside.

I jumped into my coveralls. Minutes later, the Red Cross called for me to report to my first aid station immediately. I grabbed a pen, steadied my shaking hand, and scribbled a note for my parents, knowing full well they wouldn't be returning any time soon to see it. I read it. I couldn't even read my own handwriting, I was shaking so much. I tore it up and wrote another.

I switched on the radio still tuned to KGMB. The announcer shouted, "Air attack has been made on Oahu. This is no maneuver. This is no drill. This is the real McCoy!"

My mind raced. Gordo is safe with the MacAlistairs. I knew they hadn't left for church yet. Mother's at the hospital. Dad was supposed to attend a lecture on "The Treatment of Deep Penetrating Wounds" at 9:00 a.m. in Honolulu and then meet me for church. The radio continued to scream its announcements. Stay off the streets. Do not use your telephone. The island is under enemy attack. Keep calm. Do not use your telephone. Fill your bathtub with water. Attach garden hoses. Be ready for possible fire. Stay tuned for further announcements.

I wondered about Helen, Frank, and Janet. We'd all been assigned to different field stations once we passed our first aid course. Were they biking or driving there now? What about Drew and his father? Were they at Hickam Field waiting for the B−17s to land? Oh, no. Miss Fort! Is she up in the air? Mr. Downing! Oh, God, please, not the *West Virginia*!

My mind raced. *In the event of an air raid, stay under cover. Wounded are hurt from falling shrapnel from anti-aircraft guns. If an air raid begins, do not go out-of-doors. Stay under cover. You may be seriously injured or instantly killed by falling shrapnel.*

I thought about the cloth roof on our Jeep. Falling shrapnel will go right through the roof. I couldn't think about that. I jumped in and raced to the headquarters of the Hawaii Chapter of the American Red Cross. When I got there about 8:40 a.m., there was so much confusion. Should they evacuate the women and children first? More attacks were expected. Should the workers go straight to their field assignments to set up the first aid stations?

I reported in, told them I had a Jeep, showed them my American Red Cross first aid certification card, and told them the name of my assigned first aid station. As soon as they heard the word "Jeep,"

however, I became immediately enlisted in the Motor Corps. My only training was the driving lessons Dad had given me. Those sure didn't include driving during an enemy air attack.

My first assignment was to get bandages and dressings to Tripler Army Hospital as fast as I could. Tripler was fifteen or twenty minutes away, but the streets were clogged with people running everywhere. I glanced at my watch: 9:20 a.m. The radio blared, " Another attack! Take cover immediately. Get off the streets. Now. This is no drill!"

When I slowed down at a corner, a sailor opened the door and hopped in. "I gotta get to my ship," he said. His buddy jumped on the running board and said, "Hurry!"

"I'll take you, but first we're stopping at Tripler." They argued with me, the sailor on the running board screaming in the window. I held firm. I knew what these bandages were for, and these two boys were all in one piece.

When we got to Tripler, they helped me carry the boxes of bandages up the blood-soaked steps to the hospital. It was absolute chaos there. The halls and grounds filled with wounded as the nurses began triage. An orderly grabbed the boxes and said, "We need more. We're all out. And they've just bombed Hickam Field."

Drew! Dear God, please no! I had to put Drew out of my mind. And Mother. And Dad. If I thought about it at all, I would break down and not be able to do what I needed to do.

I picked my way through the bodies of wounded soldiers and sailors laid out in the lobby and rushed down the stairs to the Jeep. I turned the key in the ignition and roared off again. My Navy hitchhikers had found another car of sailors heading to their ship. I was glad because I had one thing on my mind. More bandages. For the next several hours that's all I did — go back and forth between the hospital and Red Cross headquarters to replenish the surgical dressing supply, ferry civilian nurses in to help, and provide supplies of sulfa drugs.

By midmorning, all the stocked blood plasma supplies were

gone. The Red Cross was sending everything it had to the hospitals. The radio, my sole companion this morning, urged civilians to donate blood immediately at the Blood Bank.

At about 11:40 a.m., the radio suddenly went dead. The silence coming from the radio which I had just turned up was ominous. Later, I learned that the Army had ordered all radios off the air. They were afraid the signals they transmitted were being used by the Japanese to direct them to Oahu. I thought about KGMB being on all night last night.

This last time I came to Tripler, I was told to take the medical supplies up to the operating floor. I grabbed as many boxes as I could carry. A sailor with blood running down his arm said, "Here, let me help you with that."

"Are you crazy?" I said. "Let me help you with that!" I took a roll of sterile bandage and dressing gauze out of the box and made him sit down on the running board of the Jeep. I knelt on the ground, and in twenty seconds flat I'd dressed and bandaged the wound.

"Hey, thanks!" he replied and insisted on carrying some of the boxes up to the second floor for me. Within seconds, the supplies were whisked out of our hands.

I looked around. Halls filled with wounded men. Patients whisked into the operating room with no attention given to removing clothing around the wounds and cleaning them first. Boy, after a whole week's lesson on the importance of cleaning wounds to keep infection down, I thought that chapter must not have been written for war! Then I remembered what we learned about digital pressure. Sure, using your hand to stop the bleeding is not sanitary, but then the goal is to not lose the patient. You say you will instruct me, Lord. And teach me in the way I should go. Well, if ever there was a time for that, it's now!

I asked where I could scrub up. Someone shouted, "We're out of soap." I pushed up my sleeves and began to look around. An unconscious sailor had blood pouring from his neck. I knelt down,

ripped off the scarf from my head, and made a compress. I applied
pressure on the wound until the bleeding slowed. A nurse named Alice
came by with a clipboard. I read his name from his nameplate on the
uniform and then said, "Apparent head wound or unconsciousness due
to loss of blood. Neck puncture wound—superficial, bleeding stopped."

The nurse looked at me in surprise and told me to come with
her. I stayed with her for over an hour, numb, acting just like I'd
been trained, helping to triage the patients, applying pressure to
blood-soaked young men to stop the bleeding, creating tourniquets
out of strips of clothing, curtains, belts, anything we could find.

Another soldier helped us move some of the patients who
had died to make room for the new patients coming in by the
truckloads. I studied each face to see if it was someone I knew,
as she marked those who died to be taken away to the makeshift
morgues.

As more civilian doctors arrived, the Army medical officers who
were in surgery came out of the operating rooms. I prayed for your
father, as I worked among the wounded. Be his hiding place, Lord.
Encompass him with songs of deliverance.

Just outside the operating room, the nurse gave artificial
respiration while I applied pressure on a sailor's abdominal wound.
After five minutes, she looked at me and said, "He's gone." I looked
at the face of the bloodstained, blond boy. He didn't look any older
than me.

Ambulances and trucks outfitted with stretchers brought in new
loads of the injured. Nurse Alice and I began the triage process all
over again with each load. She, with her clipboard, and me with my
supply of bandages. Someone tossed me the keys to the Jeep, sent
back by the officers filled with wounded soldiers. The keys were
bloodstained. I shoved them into my pocket.

Nurse Alice identified those who were dying with a cross on
their forehead. They would not receive any medical treatment.
Others got an "M" if they needed morphine. I gripped the railing
as I watched her mark someone with a cross on the forehead. It was

Drew's father. He was barely conscious. "Lieutenant Masterson!" I exclaimed. Then I called for Nurse Alice. I pleaded with her with my eyes, but she shook her head and turned away. I stayed with him and held his hand. I talked to him about flying, about the wind in your face as you soar toward the heavens, until he died.

I wanted to scream, "NO!" and stop all this madness. I couldn't handle it anymore. Yet I had to handle it. There was so much more to handle. Nurse Alice called for me. I struggled to my feet with tears stinging my eyes. Resolute, I made my way over the men—wounded, dying, and dead—to catch up with her. We continued to work our way down the hall as I fought back my tears. If Drew were with him …

An half hour later, the doors swung open to the operating theater. Dad walked out, ripping a sweaty mask from his face. I couldn't believe my eyes: my father, a Navy Medical Corps surgeon, walking alongside two Army doctors. "Dad!" I shouted. "Over here." I continued to apply pressure to a young soldier's wounds.

Dad rushed to me and put his hand on my head as I knelt next to the young soldier. He knelt down with me, examined the wound, and watched me as I dressed it. I ripped the tape with my teeth as I continued to put pressure on the gaping wound with my hand. "Merrie," he said quietly when I was done, "good job."

I told Dad I had the Jeep and didn't know what to do. He said he'd been in surgery nonstop for six hours, but now he had to get to the Naval Hospital. "There're a lot of casualties there," he explained. "I'll tell you about it on the way."

The Jeep radio blasted when Dad turned the key. I explained that the radio had been off a good part of the day. The announcer reported we were now under martial law. Hawaii was under military rule now. I looked at my watch again. It was 3:25 p.m.

The rumors had spread through the hospital all day. The Japanese had invaded, were ransacking the city, and would soon take us prisoner. Earlier, I pushed each of those rumors out of my mind to do what I needed to do. Now on the ride, they came screaming back in my mind.

The highway was blocked with cars all trying to get somewhere. It took us two hours to get back to Hospital Point. By the time we got to the hospital, Dad told me what he knew. There were two attacks by the Japanese within two hours of each other. No one knows if there will be more. They hit a lot of ships, many were on fire, and some were sinking.

He was with other military and civilian doctors, gathered to hear Dr. Moorehead this morning teach on deep puncure wounds. Just as Dr. Moorehead began reading from the Bible, the doors flew open, and one of the doctors rushed in and said, "Pearl Harbor's being bombed. All doctors report to Tripler General Hospital immediately." The Scripture? "Be ye also ready, for in such an hour as ye thinketh not, the son of man cometh."

When Dad asked how I was doing, I said, "Dad ... the gaping wounds ... the arms and legs just blown off ... I ... I ..." Dad grabbed my hand and squeezed it. There was nothing more we could say. He had seen it too.

Dad began to tell me how to treat serious oil burns and flash burns, something we'd definitely not covered in our class. Suddenly, I realized what he was doing. Ships bombed. Fires. Burning oil. The wounded. He was preparing me for what was ahead. He talked to me about shock and infection. Calmly, very carefully, he went through step-by-step what to do when a patient is covered with burns.

When we arrived at the Naval Hospital, we found the grounds had become a temporary morgue. The hospital morgue and the basement of the laboratory were already filled with dead bodies. Dad looked at me and asked, "You all right?" I nodded and walked a bit faster.

We found Mother to let her know we were all right. I asked about Gordo. Mother said she got word from the MacAlistairs that Gordo's with them in the basement of the main hospital building, which is serving as an air-raid shelter. On her break, she'd go and check on him. Mother gave Dad an update of the medical situation there.

Mother saw the flight of about twenty planes go over the hospital the same time I did. When she saw the red sun on the

wings, she knew we were under attack by the Japanese. They were only about one hundred feet off the ground when they flew over. All medical officers were called. Those who lived off base arrived fairly quickly. Mother got worried when she didn't hear from Dad. Later she heard the doctors at the lecture had gone to Tripler. She said it sure was good to see him standing there in front of her.

Mother said the hospital went immediately to full alert. Staff prepared the surgical dressing centers and the operating units. They moved the ambulatory patients to tents and some old frame buildings to open up the regular wards for battle casualties. Many officers and men who were patients begged to be released to return to their commands. Most of these requests were quickly authorized.

Just like what happened at Tripler Hospital, within forty-five minutes casualties began to stream in to the Naval Hospital in ambulances, trucks, cars, delivery wagons—brought in by military and citizens alike. There were four operating units going at all times in the main hospital suite. They set up a temporary receiving station in the old nurses' quarters for minor injuries. I had to wonder, what's minor on a day like today? Most everything I'd seen at Tripler was horrific.

Mother said hundreds had been treated for serious wounds here. She explained that when the USS *Shaw*'s magazine exploded, the blast shook the hospital and shattered some windows, covering several patients with glass. The USS *Nevada* had beached on Hospital Point, and the sailors swam to shore through burning oil. She added quietly, "They've already begun to bury the dead."

Dad left to scrub for surgery. I thought about how tired both he and Mother must be. Yet you'd never know it from how they acted. Mother told me that some of the wives from Naval Housing near us came in to help, but they sure could use trained volunteers.

Mother asked me if I was ready. I breathed deep and nodded, and we were off to the wards. "Do you remember what you learned about shock?"

"Dad gave me a refresher course on the way here."

"Good, get ready. These are burn patients. It's going to be tough." Then she pushed open the door to the ward.

Mother had me come with her as she took a flit gun from the stock and filled it with tannic acid to cool the burns. She taught me how to spray the solution. Together, like this, we worked for hours. I sprayed burned bodies as she gave the most severely wounded patients morphine shots for the pain.

At dark, some staff hammered up black drapes and black paper to make sure no light came from the hospital. This time the blackout was for real. The radio playing low droned on, "Please turn out your lights ... Hawaii is observing a complete blackout. Turn out your lights. This means the whole Territory. Turn out your lights, and do not turn them on for any purpose whatsoever. Turn off your lights and keep them off." Then once again, the radio went silent.

We continued to work in the dark with flashlights covered with blue cellophane. The complete darkness. The silence from the radio. The groans from the patients. I pushed my hair out of my face and realized how many times this day I had some soldier's or sailor's lifeblood on those same hands.

About 10:00 p.m., we heard planes overhead and gunfire. We all stood still, waiting. One of the men cried out, "Nurse, nurse!" I knew he was scared. So was I. I held his bandaged hand and prayed with him. Thou art my hiding place. Soon it was silent. Later we found out those were our planes with our own guys shooting at them. Everyone is on edge and expecting the Japanese back at any time.

Finally, Mother and I took a break. We stepped over people stretched out wall to wall who were trying to sleep in the basement air-raid shelter. We found Gordo lying on his blanket. Mother knelt down, and he grabbed her neck and wouldn't let go. I told her I would stay with him until he got back to sleep. I laid down beside him and cuddled him in my arms until he dozed off. Then it was back to the wards.

The next day, Mother and Gordo and I walked home, arm in arm. Mother took a shower first, then me. Gordo worked on finding material to black out the windows. Dad came home just long enough to shower and change. We filled up every pot and jar with water. Before Dad went back to the hospital, he asked us to all come to the living room.

We gathered around the radio to listen to the president ask Congress for a declaration of war against Japan. He said what we all knew yesterday—we're at war. We knelt down and said a prayer for all those who were wounded or killed. We prayed for our friends. I prayed for your father's protection. We haven't heard from him yet, and I know you must be terrified too.

I prayed for Drew and his family. I can't shake the image of his father at Tripler. I hope Drew's safe. I prayed for my flight instructor, Miss Fort, who I knew was supposed to give a lesson the same time the attack began. Dad had told me he heard private planes had been shot down, but he didn't know if one of them was Miss Fort's plane. We prayed for Mr. and Mrs. Downing, and the young men we know from the *West Virginia* that had sung, and laughed, and prayed with us in this very living room. Then we prayed for the many young men from all these burning, sinking ships. *Father forgive.*

Your friend,

Merrie

Washington, D.C.

DECEMBER 8, 1941

Dear Merrie,

Are you okay? Your family? Have you had any word about Daddy? Can you find out for us? We're desperate for news. Mom didn't go to work today, and I'm trying to find out what I can from the newspaper. One of Mom's Navy friends got a telegram to let her know her husband is okay, but we've heard nothing from Daddy. Please, see what you and your parents can do to help us. I'm so scared.

We don't know much here. On Sunday, I was at Griffith Stadium for the Redskins-Eagles game with Mr. Ward and his son. In the middle of the game, Mr. Ward seemed distracted. He was listening to the announcements on the public address system. *All military personnel report to your posts. General Abrams, call your office. Ambassador to the Philippines, contact your office.* The announcements continued. *All* Washington Times Herald *staff, report to your office immediately.* Mr. Ward leaned over, "They called the *Herald* in. Something's up, kid, and it's big. I'm sorry. We've got to go." When Mr. Ward came back from the press box, we knew Japan had bombed Pearl Harbor.

On the trolley back to the office, all I could think about was Daddy, and you and your family. When we came through the door to the paper, the phones were jangling and reporters were already typing. "Murray, here, read this wire!" *At 7:55 a.m. Hawaiian time, the Japanese bombed Pearl Harbor.* Mr. McGurdy shouted out orders: "Call the White House. See if you can get a confirmation. What's the police radio say? Has anybody got ahold of Hal yet?"

I called Mom and told her where I was. She'd already heard on the radio. Mom said for me to stay at the paper. I was more likely to hear something before she would. "Mom?" I said. "Daddy ..." His name caught in my throat. A million fears rushed through my mind and gripped my heart.

She responded, "I know, Catherine, just pray. And let me know if you hear anything. I'll call Hank."

Mr. McGurdy sent me over to the White House to see what I could pick up from outside the gates. He had other reporters working their connections to the inside. "Human interest, Clark," he reminded me. It helped to be busy. On my way out, Mr. Ward said, "I'll call your mother if I hear anything about Kaneohe."

I walked to Pennsylvania Avenue to the front lawn of the White House. Hundreds of people stood outside the iron picket fence, waiting, wanting news. Although clumped in groups, they stood silent, watching, willing the president to do something. Soldiers, in uniform, hurried by me. Congressmen arrived in black cars. A Navy officer arrived with an attaché case.

I took notes as fast as I could, but what I really wanted to do was rush up to each one and beg them to tell me if they had news of my daddy. When I got back to the office, I gave the notes to Mr. Ward. He said, "Kaneohe was hit hard. Don't know about casualties yet, but, kid ..." It was the way he said it that scared me. "I've called your mother and told her. She wants you to come home."

I gathered up my things. Mr. Ward added, "Keep your chin up. It'll be awhile before any of us know the whole story. I'm sure you'll hear from your father soon." I made him promise to call us with any news.

When I got home, I fell into Mom's arms. We both cried a year's worth of tears in the next hour. I pray Daddy's okay. And your parents. And you and Gordon. So many people I love are right there in Pearl Harbor. We kept the radio on for news. The announcer introduced Mrs. Roosevelt. Mom grabbed her shorthand pad and a pen to take notes for me. Here's what she said, in case you didn't hear her. "I am speaking to you tonight at a very serious moment in our history. The Cabinet is convening and the leaders in Congress are meeting with the president ... By tomorrow morning the members of Congress will have a full report and be ready for action ... I should like to say just a word to the women in the country tonight. I have a boy at sea on a destroyer, and for all I know he may be on his way to the Pacific. Many of you all over the country have boys in the services who will now be called upon to go into action. You have friends and families in what has suddenly become a danger zone. You cannot escape anxiety. You cannot escape a clutch of fear at your heart, and yet I hope that the certainty of what we have to meet will make you rise above these fears.

"To the young people of the nation, I must speak a word tonight. You are going to have a great opportunity. There will be high moments in which your strength and your ability will be tested. I have faith in you. I feel as though I am standing upon a rock and that rock is my faith in my fellow citizens."

Mom said quietly, "It'll take more than faith in fellow citizens to get us through this." I noticed she was still clutching her Bible verse card that Daddy had sent to her. *Yea, though I walk though the valley of the shadow of death, I will fear no evil; for thou art with me.*

This morning, Mom went to work to learn what she could at the White House. She sent me back to the paper. I didn't want to go to school anyway. I'm desperate for news about Daddy and what's happening.

At the *Chronicle*, I ran copy, I glued articles for composing, and I got coffee for the guys. At 12:30 p.m., we all stopped what we were doing to hear President Roosevelt address the joint session of Congress: "Yesterday, December 7, 1941 — a date which will live in infamy — the United States of America was suddenly and deliberately attacked by naval and air forces of the Empire of Japan … There is no blinking at the fact that our people, our territory, and our interests are in grave danger … I ask that the Congress declare that since the unprovoked and dastardly attack by Japan on Sunday, December seventh, a state of war has existed between the United States and the Japanese Empire."

A day which will live in infamy. I pray a day that Mom and I will not remember as the worst of our lives. We have no word. We still hope.

Your friend,

Catherine

Pearl Harbor, Hawaii

December 10, 1941

Dear Catherine,

I know you must be sick with worry about your father. By now, you've received our telegram and should know we're safe and looking for your father.

Dad found out that the Naval Air Station at Kaneohe lost most of the patrol planes when both the airstrip and the hangars were strafed by the Japanese in two different attacks. Dad said there were fires there, and a lot of casualties. I asked Dad which hospital they'd be taken to, but he said with all the confusion, the wounded might be taken anywhere care could be given — even makeshift wards. It might take days or weeks to sort it all out.

I had to try to find out something about your father. I worked with the clerks at the front desk of the Naval Hospital and eliminated some of the hospitals. I already knew from my rounds yesterday that he isn't here. Dad's fairly sure he isn't on the hospital ship USS *Solace* because most of those wounded were from the ships. The best bet is to start with the dispensary at the Kaneohe Naval Air Station. I'll have to wait until Dad can go with me.

My parents are both working pretty much around the clock at the hospital. Mother arranged for Gordo to stay with the MacAlistairs so I could help out at the hospital too. Yesterday, I took three-by-five-inch cards and pencils around to the men. If they could write, they could send a short note to their families to let them know they were okay. They can't say anything about the attack, though. I wondered what else they could write about on such a small card. As I thought about your father, I thought how much it would mean to you and your mother just to receive a card in his own handwriting with the words: "I'm okay."

That made me determined to help those patients whose hands were too burned to write. I wrote whatever they told me, writing as small as possible to crowd as many words on the card as I could. I was careful not to include anything they said about the attack, the names of ships or places. I didn't want their card set aside by the censors. On the other side of the card, I wrote the man's name, his rank, his command, and the address of his family.

I won't give up, I promise. I'm going to find your father.

Your friend,

Mettie

Washington, D.C.

December 10, 1941

Dear Merrie,

We got your telegram. We're so glad you're safe! Thank you for looking for Daddy. At least he's not at the Naval Hospital, or you'd know. I guess that's good news. But why hasn't he tried to reach us? Mom tells me not to let my mind go to the worst, but it's hard not to. I didn't want to go to school in case there was word, but Mom said it could be awhile before we know about Daddy. She wants us to continue our routine. We've declared war against the Japanese. Daddy's missing. This is anything but routine!

At school, all anyone can talk about is the war. We had a long assembly to learn the procedures for an air raid drill. Right after the assembly, we had our first drill. The entire building was evacuated in ten minutes. Western High is now a designated air raid shelter for the community. Teachers are air raid wardens and will take turns sleeping here at night to guard the building.

At the *Breeze* office, we sorted through bulletins from the Office of Civilian Defense and the Board of Education. Instructions on evacuating the building, air raid drills, sirens and signals, air raid shelters, aviation courses, and how to graduate early to enlist were scattered all over the table. I stared at all the pamphlets. Not one of them explained how to find a missing father.

Some students didn't return to Western, but signed up for the service. We've heard some of our men teachers may leave to join the service too. Robert pulled me aside and told me he's decided to graduate early in February. He smiled. "But maybe we can dance at Glen Echo before I go." It's strange, but with Daddy, it's like everything's in slow motion, but with everything else, it's going so fast I feel weak.

Your friend,

Catherine

Pearl Harbor, Hawaii

DECEMBER 12, 1941

Dear Catherine,

They released lists from Kaneohe NAS. He's not on the injured list, and he's not on the list of dead either. Your father is missing. I'm sorry to tell you this, but I know you'd want to know whatever we find out. I'll keep looking. Dad's sending your mom a telegram today. I wish we had better news.

Today, I went to the Coconut Shack to meet Helen and Frank. On the way there, I saw Janet. I called out to her. "Janet." She didn't hear me. I shouted louder, "Miyoko, hello!"

She looked horrified. She rushed to me, grabbed my arm, and demanded, "You must call me Janet." She told me her father had been picked up by the police the same night as the bombing. She hasn't seen him since. Her mother's terrified. Miyoko, I mean Janet, speaks to her in Japanese but cannot reassure her. Military officers went through their house and carried out her father's ceremonial sword, his shortwave radio, and a box of his papers. The next day Janet found the Japanese Language School boarded up.

I didn't know what to say except how sorry I was. She spoke quietly, and turned and walked away. Her words rang in my head: "I am an American too."

As Janet hurried away, I thought of all the rumors that had swept this island over the last week. Some said arrows cut in sugarcane fields led the bombers to the ships. Or the Japanese signaled the bombers in advertisements which ships to hit. A Japanese flier who was shot down wore a McKinley High School ring. A Japanese ad that said, "Fashions by the Yard: Look at Our Silks on Parade," signaled the plan to attack the Navy Yard. "Parade" really meant air raid, and "Silks" come from Japan; therefore, Japanese Air Raid! Then I heard Janet's words to me as I watched her walk away: "I am an American too."

The Coconut Shack was closed. Frank and Helen and I sat at a picnic table and told each other about Attack Day. Frank said there were lots of civilian injuries brought into his station. He shuddered as he recalled a young girl who was hit by a piece of shrapnel. I told them about helping out at Tripler Hospital that day and the days since at the Naval Hospital. I tried to tell them about seeing Drew's father right before he died, but stopped. It seemed wrong to talk about it without Drew there, even though they'd heard about his father. Frank told me that Hickam was totally bombed out, and that Drew and his mother had moved in with some friends in Honolulu. Helen's father has been hurt badly and may be on the first ship out of here to the mainland.

Frank heard several civilian pilots who were up in the air at the time of the attack were killed, but he didn't have any names. All civilian pilots are grounded now. You can only get to John Rodgers Airport with a special military pass now. I don't know any other way to contact Miss Fort. I pray she's okay.

After lunch, we went to the Blood Bank to make an appointment to donate blood. The lines are down the street. There's talk about evacuating all the women and children back to the mainland. Tonight Mother asked me to start packing up what Gordo and I would need for school clothes in San Francisco. We'll stay with Granddaddy. Mother wants our suitcases packed and our school transfer papers in order.

It's still not clear if she'll come with us. Dad will definitely stay. I don't want to go. I want to stay here, find your father, talk to Drew about his father, see if Miss Fort's okay, and keep our family together. We have no idea when we have to go. At a moment's notice, the life here I have come to know and love could be ripped out of my hands.

The blackouts continue. Our home has blankets at some windows and black paint on others. Dad put blue film over his headlights for when he's out at night. Hitler declared war on the United States today, and Dad came home last night with gas masks for each of us. Some Christmas present.

Your friend,

Merrie

Pearl Harbor, Hawaii

December 16, 1941

Dear Catherine,

I've been working with one of the chaplains to try to find your father. He checks the hospital records each day because they move the wounded around to different hospitals. Some injured men have no identification and are unconscious. I make the rounds of the new patients here to see if I recognize your father.

Mr. Downing stopped by today to visit one of his shipmates who was transferred here. I gave him a huge hug. Dad told me he'd heard Mr. and Mrs. Downing were fine, but boy, to see him and hug him ... None of us made it to Sunday school that morning, so it felt so good. I can't wait to do that with your father.

Mr. and Mrs. Downing stayed in Honolulu Saturday night at the DeGroff's home where the Navigators often meet. Mr. Downing was getting ready for our Sunday school class when explosions shook the house. He told me that as he jumped in the car to head back to his ship, he'll never forget the sight of Morena. He had no idea if he would ever see her again. She called out a verse from the Bible to him as he drove off. "The eternal God is thy refuge, and underneath are the everlasting arms."

He told me he prayed for his high school Bible students that morning as he sped towards the ship. He thought about us, where we were, if we were safe. I gave him an extra hug when he said that. I'd sure needed prayer that morning!

When he finally got to Ford Island, the *West Virginia* rested on the bottom in forty feet of water and was jammed against the *Tennessee*. "Just a hundred feet away flames from the burning *Arizona* leaped skyward while the oil floating on the water caught fire," he explained. "Sailors were trying to swim through that inferno. We worked for a couple of hours to get all of the wounded to shore for help."

When I asked Mr. Downing how he felt during that time, his answer didn't surprise me. He said that his heart was flooded with peace. God's peace in the midst of danger. A peace that makes no sense otherwise. I remembered my time at Tripler and at the Naval Hospital. I remembered the smell of burning flesh and the eerie silence of sailors willing to wait their turn for medical attention. I remembered the men asking for help for their buddies, even when they needed help themselves. I remembered being numb and yet strangely at peace the whole time. I hugged Mr. Downing again.

It's the week before Christmas. There're no Christmas trees or Christmas presents coming from the mainland. Boats are reserved for wounded, evacuation, and supplies. The Aloha Tower is painted with camouflage paint instead of its usual Christmas decorations. Waikiki Beach is covered in barbed wire to protect us in case the enemy lands on the beaches. The white sand is covered with oil spilled from the ships.

Christmas lights put up before Attack Day were taken down. Instead of Christmas carols reminding us of peace on earth, we have air raid sirens telling us it is war.

Your friend,

Merrie

Pearl Harbor, Hawaii

DECEMBER 18, 1941

Dear Catherine,

I made my rounds today as usual at the Naval Hospital with cards and pencils. Gordo came with me just in case anyone wanted to borrow from his stack of comic books. Lieutenant Bender at the front desk told me there were seven transferees and which wards they were in. He knows how hard I'm trying to find your father.

Gordo got to talking to one sailor who loves Captain Midnight almost as much as he does. I left them comparing notes on the latest episode and went to see the new transferees. Today, I saw a man who seemed oddly familiar. Was it the tilt of his head? The color of his hair? I wasn't sure. He was heavily bandaged. Even his face was covered in bandages. I assumed he must have severe burns. His left arm had been amputated. The more I stood there and prayed for him, the more I became convinced I knew him. Could he be your father?

I flew back down to the front desk. "Sir, I think it's Lieutenant Clark!"

"Did you recognize him?"

"No, sir, he's too heavily bandaged, but there's just something about him. Please, can you check? Hurry!"

Yes, the patient was from Kaneohe NAS! He had been treated initially at the dispensary there, and later transferred with about forty men to the Kaneohe Territorial Hospital for the Insane, the closest hospital. Yesterday, he was stable enough to be transferred here. There are several seriously wounded patients that we know are from Kaneohe NAS who are not yet identified. Lieutenant Bender said, "It's been tough to identify everyone who was killed or missing or even injured. It's a process, you know."

"Could it be Lieutenant Clark?"

"It's possible."

I ran to find Dad, who was on duty, and brought him to the bedside of this man. Dad took one look and said, "I think it's Wes."

Dad made a phone call to the chaplain who came right away. He told us that identification by fingerprints has been difficult because so many men had their fingers burned. Dad gently unwrapped the bandage on the right arm. His fingers were badly burned, but they were able to get a partial print from one of his fingers. We'd know soon!

The hours went by interminably slow. Then we got the news. It's your father! He's here at the Naval Hospital with Dad looking after him. He's going to be okay. Dad immediately sent a telegram to your mother, which I know you've read by now. Dad said to tell you he'll watch over him like a brother.

I'm so happy for you!

Your friend,

Merrie

Washington, D.C.

DECEMBER 19, 1941

Dear Merrie,

Mom and I celebrated last night. Dad's alive! I ache to know he's so badly wounded, but the joy of knowing he's alive and will return to us is enough. Mom went to Western Union this morning before work to send Hank a telegram. Thank you for not giving up. It might have been weeks more before we knew anything. Please give Daddy a hug for me. Here's a letter to give to him. You should have seen me today at school and at the *Chronicle*. I was dancing around!

The *Breeze* came out today packed with hard news. I never thought I would see the day! Not one word on fashion. Only a small story on football, and a notice that the Christmas Candlelight Ball has been canceled. Instead, there are pages and pages on blackouts, air raids, and national defense. I picked up a couple of extra issues to show the men at the *Chronicle*.

Washington is set to have its first citywide air raid drill in two days. This afternoon, at the *Chronicle*, Mr. McGurdy said, "Clark, I want you to double-team with Ward on this air raid thing. Your school's a shelter, isn't it? You get me the story, and I'll get you the byline."

"Yes, sir!"

I've been working all day on background. The OCD Bulletins I'd sorted through for the *Breeze* put me miles ahead.

I think we've both found what we love to do. You'll be a famous aviatrix, and I'll cover your climb into the history books as you break records and confound audiences with your daring-do!

Your friend,

Catherine

Honolulu, Hawaii

DECEMBER 25, 1941

Dear Catherine,

What a strange Christmas Day! We reported to the pier this afternoon to the SS *Lurline*, the ocean liner turned military transport ship that will take us to the mainland.

The last time the SS *Lurline* loaded up her passengers was on December 5th, two days before Attack Day. Helen, Frank, Drew, and I came down to the pier that day to see that beautiful ship set sail in the late afternoon. We climbed the eight-story Aloha Tower to the observation deck. All white and gleaming, she set sail as the Royal Hawaiian Hotel band played and hula girls danced. Local boys dove for coins thrown from the top deck. The smell of plumeria and sweet mountain maile leis filled the air.

Carrying white parasols, the ladies wore white cotton dresses and white gloves. Naval officers in dress whites and civilians in crisp linen suits strolled along with them. These were the *passengers*. Each one of these 800 passengers was a celebrity. Among them were military wives and children returning to the States because worried spouses feared that the conflict with Japan was heating up.

We should have realized it then, but on that day three weeks ago, Frank, Helen, Drew, and I wanted to forget. We wanted to forget preparedness classes, first aid instructions, blackout drills, and the worried looks of our parents. We stood on the observation deck of the Aloha Tower and watched the SS *Lurline* sail smoothly out of the harbor as the band played on.

Now the once-white SS *Lurline* is camouflaged with gray paint and stripped of its luxury conditions. When it sets sail, four destroyers and a light cruiser will go along. And instead of white dresses and gloves, we'll wear life preservers over our clothes at all times — just in case.

Mother walked around the house, organizing everything, making sure we had all we need for the trip. She checked her list against the things in Gordo's suitcase. She packed it, then unpacked it, then packed it again. When she came to my room, I said, "Mother, it's all here. It's fine."

She sat down on my bed. I sat next to her. She brushed away a tear, smoothed her uniform, then smoothed my hair away from my eyes. "I don't know how long ..."

"We'll be fine, Mother. I'll take care of Gordon. I promise."

"You'd make a very good nurse, you know. I was never so proud of you as on that day." Her voice trailed off as she gazed out the window toward the Naval Hospital. Then she continued, "But I know you want to be a pilot. I'm sure you'll be a great one. You're very brave." We hugged each other for a very long time.

Gordo rode his bike to his friends' houses to tell them good-bye. Helen and her family left on a ship last week. They sent her father to San Francisco for more surgery. We promised to find each other once we get there. I called Frank, and we promised to write. He leaves next week. Gwendolyn and I said our good-byes awhile back. I couldn't take any more of her hysterics and the "I told you so" tirades about the Japanese.

Then I called Drew. We met for the last time at the Coconut Shack for lunch (nothing's opened at night anymore), but neither of us felt much like eating. He told me the Japanese killed his flight instructor, Bob Tyce, at John Rodgers Airport, when it strafed the hangars. I asked him if he'd heard anything about Miss Fort and Miss Guild. He heard they were okay, but Miss Fort had been up in the air during the attack. When a Japanese plane came right at her, she had to grab the controls away from her student and jam the throttle wide open to pull above the oncoming plane. She began her descent with machine-gun fire after her. She got the plane down safely and her student didn't even realize what was happening! I gave Drew a note to give to her for me.

He told me he'll help his mother get things settled before she returns to the mainland. Roosevelt High may let him graduate early so he can enlist. All those flight hours and credits earned in the aviation course will mean something now. Drew says he has a score to settle.

I hugged him good-bye, and we promised to write. Somehow, I know we'll probably never see each other again. I thanked him for being a good friend and thought of what might have been.

I tried to call Miyoko, but her phone line is dead. Good-bye, Janet, my American friend.

Dad got off duty in time to drive us to the pier. He put both hands on my shoulders and gave me last-minute instructions. "Keep this money safe. You have Granddaddy's phone number? He'll meet you when the ship gets in. Watch over Gordon." He hugged me extra tight this time, then put his strong hands back on my shoulders. "There's no flying here for civilians and won't be for a very long time. Perhaps once you get settled in San Francisco, if the war permits, you can resume your flying lessons. I'd like to see you do that." I hugged him so tight I thought his uniform buttons would pop off. His strong arms felt so good around me. I didn't want him to let go. I wanted to remember that hug for a long, long time.

"Sailor man," he said to Gordo, "shipping off now?"

"Aye, aye, sir," Gordo said with a quick salute.

"Take care of your sister, sailor man."

Mother hugged us and gave Gordo a kiss which he didn't wipe off. She hugged me, kissed my cheek, and brushed my hair out of my face again. I smiled, knowing her fussing over me was her way of letting me go. Gordo and I walked up the gangplank, then turned around to wave good-bye. Dad had his arms around Mother, who looked more like a child there tucked under Dad's strong arm.

It's okay, Mother. I know exactly how you feel. Merry Christmas, Mother. Merry Christmas, Dad.

Merry Christmas, Catherine.

Your friend,

Merrie

Washington, D.C.

DECEMBER 25, 1941

Dear Merrie,

Last night Mom and I went over to the White House for the lighting of the National Christmas Tree. Mrs. Roosevelt made sure Mom had passes for us to be close to the front. The president said our patriotism, love of freedom, or even national courage is not enough. He reminded us we need God's guidance to be able to be humble and thankful and to endure sacrifice. Only then will we be brave enough to achieve a victory of liberty and peace. I'll never forget what he said: "Against enemies who preach the principles of hate and practice them, we set our faith in human love and in God's care for us and all men everywhere."

The crowd gasped as a surprise guest stepped from the South Portico to join President Roosevelt. It was Winston Churchill, the Prime Minister of Great Britain. He stepped to the microphone and encouraged all of us, who now have experienced what his country has so long endured, to remember that Christmas Day is a day of peace and joy, and that we will work together to protect the right to live in a free and decent world.

Mom and I stood in the cold, arms around each other, and thought of all we had to celebrate this night knowing Daddy's alive. It was his card to Hank that meant the most to us tonight. He wrote, "Don't worry. It wasn't my pitching arm. You get ready to run. And I'll be there to pitch to you."

The president flipped the switch and the Christmas tree, a symbol of peace and hope, lit up the sky in front of a White House with blackout drapes.

When we got home, I gave Mr. McGurdy a call — at home. "Sir," I said, "have I got a scoop for you!"

Your friend,

Catherine

Aboard the SS Lurline

DECEMBER 31, 1941

Dear Catherine,

We're supposed to arrive in San Francisco tomorrow. The ship has zigged and zagged to avoid detection from possible Japanese submarines. The portholes are covered with black paint. We have to wear life preservers over our clothes at all times. Gordo can't go anywhere without me or an adult. There are no radios permitted, no cameras, and no movies. We get no news and certainly no word on the war.

It's the end of a year I'll never forget. And it's the beginning of a new year. A time for hope when all seems lost. A time to shout out the words, whether with pain and agony, like Drew; or with fear and concern, like Miyoko; or with hope and expectancy, like us:

FATHER, FORGIVE!

Your friend,

Merrie

Epilogue

December 7, 1941, changed life abruptly for all Americans.
One day later, the United States declared war on Japan, and on
December 11, Germany and Italy declared war on the United
States. Whether one lived in the Territory of Hawaii where the
attack on America occurred, in the nation's capital, or in the
heartland of America, students felt the impact of this world war.

Honolulu after 1941

Life in Paradise changed radically for the high school student.
Schools remained closed until February 1942, and some students
never returned. Some graduated early and entered the military.
Others moved to the mainland due to the forced evacuations of
military children. Students who remained had to register and be
fingerprinted along with everyone else on the island. Students
carried gas masks with them wherever they went. They marched
into trenches dug in school yards during air-raid drills. Real air
raids, first aid classes, gas and food rationing, censorship, and
martial law were a part of everyday life in Hawaii.

Enemy torpedo attacks on ships in the area increased the sense
of vulnerability and the fear that the island would be attacked
again. On March 4, 1942, two Japanese bombers flew over Oahu.
The planes missed Pearl Harbor but dropped bombs less than
a mile from Roosevelt High School. Young men at Roosevelt
graduated early to enlist. Roosevelt girls worked with the Office of
Civilian Defense to produce over 70,000 gas masks for children by
the summer of 1942.

Western High School, Washington, D.C.

Rear Admiral Husband E. Kimmell, the Navel Commander in
Chief of the U.S. Fleet and the Pacific Fleet, and a graduate from

Western High (class of 1900) faced one of the greatest challenges of his career at Pearl Harbor. Another Westerner, Captain Joseph K. Taussig, Jr., was the senior officer in charge on the USS *Nevada* on December 7, 1941. A corporal in Company K of the Western High Cadets in 1936, Captain Taussig refused to leave his station on the USS *Nevada*, although severely wounded. He was awarded the Navy Cross for his actions. Mildred Fish-Harnack, a 1919 graduate of Western High, was active in Germany in the resistance movement. Hitler personally ordered her execution in 1943.

In December 1941, Western High students, like the rest of America, found life defined by the war. In early 1942, students gathered 7,000 books for soldiers in the nationwide Victory Book Drive, more than any other high school in the country. Each book had a sticker inside that read, "bearing the love and loyalty of the boys and girls of the Western High School." The Western High War Bond drive over the next two years raised enough funds to purchase eleven Jeeps and one training plane. Guest speakers at school assemblies included members of the military and veterans of battles.

Western High courses changed as well. In conjunction with the Army Map Center, the school offered a course in mapmaking. In the mechanical drawing course, boys made model airplanes built to military specifications to train airplane spotters. The school changed its aviation and radio courses to meet military requirements. The school adopted Army and Navy standards for physical fitness classes. All students took nutrition courses, as it was considered a patriotic duty to eat right.

Before the Pearl Harbor attack, the school paper, the *Western Breeze*, reported on sports, dances, fashion, club meetings, and Cadet competitions. By 1943, Western High records noted: "With the progress of the war, the *Breeze* has come to think of itself as one of the major war activities of the school. Unless the paper can function in this capacity, there is no excuse for using in war time the materials, time, and energy that go into the making of a school newspaper." Reporters' assignment sheets included articles about air raids; victory gardens; food and gas ration books; scrap metal, paper, tinfoil, and rubber drives; sales of war bonds and stamps; sending boxes to prisoners of war at Thanksgiving; first aid training; and interviews with men on furlough and war refugees. And school dances? Well, the Glen Miller band broke up in fall 1942 when its leader, Glen Miller, enlisted in the Army.

One popular column in the *Breeze*, "Westerners at War," kept track of Western students in the military. By 1943, there were at least 1,123 Western alumnae on the comprehensive list, and sixteen of those were young women. The Civil Air Patrol Cadets, part of the Air Division of the Victory Corps, had at least three Western girls taught to fly by Western High aviation teacher Mrs. Robinson. And two female students of Mrs. Robinson wrote the "Flight Log" column about aviation in the *Western Breeze*. In 1943, after just eight hours of instruction, Western High senior Kathryn Atema soloed in a Piper Cub and proclaimed her ambition to become a WASP. Interestingly, although a pilot, she had never learned to drive due to the gas rationing.

WAFS/WASP Pilots

Many girls yearned to fly in service for their country. The waiting list to become a WASP (Women's Airforce Service Pilot) was long and competition fierce. Over 25,000 young women applied, but only 1,830 were selected for the training program, and only 1,074 of them graduated. In September 1942, Nancy Love founded the WAFS (Women's Auxiliary Flying Squadron) comprised of twenty-eight young women who had at least 500 hours of flight time. (Only 200 hours were required for men). Cornelia Fort, the third to sign up, arrived at New Castle, Delaware, for training in September 1942. Jackie Cochran

returned from England, having proved American women could ferry planes for England, and formed the 319th Women's Flying Training Detachment; its first class began in November 1942. In August 1943, the military combined these two women's flying squadrons into the WASP. Thirty-eight women pilots died during World War II, including Cornelia Fort. On March 21, 1943, she became the first woman pilot to die in service to her country.

Now the Lord is Spirit; and where the spirit of the Lord is, there is liberty.
2 Corinthians 3:17

Dear Reader,

When I wrote Liberty Letters, I intended to communicate America's journey of freedom and also to illustrate the personal faith journey of girls who made bold choices to help others, and in doing so, helped shape the course of history. Through their stories, we learn the facts, customs, lifestyles of days gone by, and so much more.

The girls I wrote about didn't consider themselves part of "history." Few people do. These were ordinary girls, going about their lives when challenging times occurred in the communities in which they lived. They discovered integrity, courage, hope, and faith within themselves as they met these challenges with creativity and innovation. American history is steeped with just these kinds of people. These people embody liberty.

Many compared the September 11, 2001, terrorist attack on the United States to the attack on Pearl Harbor sixty years before. Now, like teenagers did years ago, you live with uncertainty. Security is tighter at airports and government buildings. In the Washington, D.C., area, military jets patrol our skies at times of heightened alert.

Sometimes, we also face challenges from what happens in our own lives or to those we love. When I grew up in Atlanta, Georgia, our good friend Hank lived across the street. He often got the neighborhood kids together for a fast-paced game of baseball. Overnight, Hank was stricken with polio and paralyzed. A hush went through our neighborhood as the news spread. We saw the fear in our parents' eyes. This was the fourth case of polio on our street in six months. Mom took us to Warm Springs to visit Hank every other weekend. While he was immobilized in an iron lung, he talked to us by looking at our reflection in the small mirror placed on the machine above his head. Later we watched him swim in the pool and, with the help of crutches and braces, take a step or two. We cheered these victories of Hank's as much as we had his home runs.

When we face challenges like these, we learn, as Catherine and Merrie did, that courage, faith, friendship, and love transform even the toughest of times into miracles of grace and give us hope for the future.

Your friend,

Nancy LeSourd

United States Air Force Museum, Wright-Patterson AFB, Dayton, Ohio

Women's Auxiliary Ferrying Squadron

Women's Auxiliary Ferrying Squadron pilots transport planes to military air bases, 1942. Cornelia Fort is second from the left.

Photo by David E. Scherman\Time Life Pictures\Getty Images

"Fifinella"
Mascot of the Women's Auxiliary Ferry Squadron

"You can be whatever you set your heart and head to be, and don't let anyone tell you you can't be, because 1,078 women pilots did it in World War II."
—Annelle Henderson Bulechek, WASP, 44-W-2

Junior Red Cross

"The foundation being laid for these boys and girls in the Junior Red Cross, which has for its motto, 'I serve,' may well be an important factor in the future welfare of our nation."
—President Franklin D. Roosevelt

National Archives

Fly Overs

American bombers fly over Waikiki Beach, Oahu, Hawaii, 1940. Women's Auxiliary Ferrying Squadron pilots transport planes to military air bases, 1942. Cornelia Fort is second from the left.

The Western Breeze, December 19, 1941

Western High School, Washington, D.C., 1941

Warm Springs

Warm Springs Foundation polio patients welcome President Roosevelt. November 29, 1941, Warm Springs, GA.

President's Birthday Ball

Eleanor Roosevelt attends the President's Birthday Ball, January 30, 1941, Washington, D.C.

PBNY 5-7-41 20M
Original

U. S. NAVAL AIR STATION, KODIAK, ALASKA
NAVAL COMMUNICATIONS

Heading	NPG NR 63 F L Z F5L 071830 C8Q TART O BT		
From:	CINCPAC		Date 7 DEC 41
To:	ALL SHIPS PRESENT AT HAWAIIN AREA.		
Info:	– U R G E N T –		
DEFERRED unless otherwise checked	ROUTINE............	PRIORITY............	AIRMAIL............

AIRRAID ON PEARLHARBOR X THIS IS NO DRILL

Naval Communication, December 7, 1941

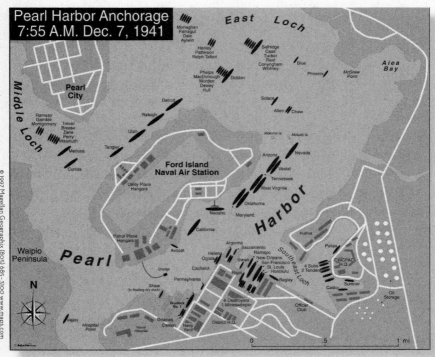

Pearl Harbor Anchorage
7:55 A.M. Dec. 7, 1941

The Attack

Rescuing survivors near USS *West Virginia*, December 7, 1941.

Wing of a Japanese bomber shot down on the grounds of the Naval Hospital during the attack on Pearl Harbor, December 7, 1941.

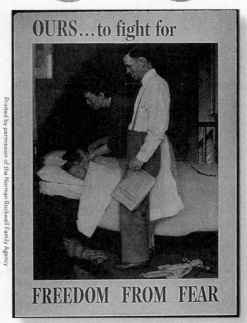

Going to War

President Roosevelt signs the Declaration of War against Japan,
December 8, 1941.

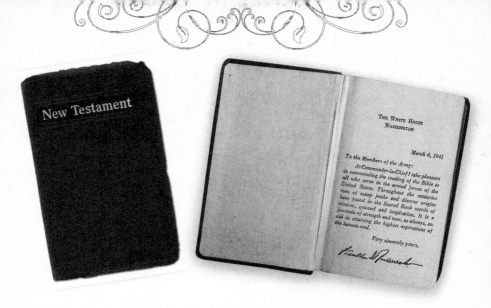

President Roosevelt's Gift to Soldiers

Air Raid Warden Handbook,
U.S. Office of Civilian Defense, 1941

Gas Masks
Hawaiian students carry gas masks
with them at all times, 1942

War Bonds
Western High students sell war bonds to
assist the war effort, 1942.

War Ration Book
Citizens purchase
sugar and gasoline
with ration stamps
during the war.

...we here highly resolve that these dead shall not have died in vain...

REMEMBER DEC. 7th!

Office of War Information, 1942

Liberty Letters

Adventures in Jamestown

kidz

Nancy LeSourd

London, England

JUNE 12, 1609

Dearest Abigail,

If I were not at the harbor myself to tell you good-bye, I would not believe my dearest friend in the entire world is gone. I stayed and watched until your ship, the *Blessing*, and the other eight ships sailed out of sight.

You always were the first to try new things, but I never thought you would leave your homeland to travel to such an unknown land, and you are just twelve! I wish I could go with you.

My brother, John, could not take his eyes off the six horses and two mares that the captain ordered hoisted up in the air and over the edge of the pier onto the *Blessing*. Interesting company for your journey! One day you can tell your grandchildren you sailed the seas with Virginia's first horses.

However, for the life of me, I cannot understand how Temperance Flowerdew is going to make it in the New World. She is fearful of her very shadow. Now I know you do not like her much, but she is one of the few girls your age, and you will need her company. With that in mind, I gave her a grand farewell as she boarded her ship, the *Falcon*.

But why is it Temperance who will share your adventures and not I? I wish Papa had decided we could go too. Mother reminds me that she and Papa have plans for me that include a proper marriage to an educated and propertied gentleman of their choosing as soon as I am old enough. But I am only thirteen now—marriage is years away. In the meantime, I am to learn the "necessary accomplishments"—the ladylike arts of needlework and music—so that I may become a suitable prospect.

If only I could go to this New World with you. Perhaps we could make it into one where girls, not just boys, study things necessary to the building of the New World. Perhaps we could even go to

school like John does. I say we establish a new law for the colony (and for all those left in London who wish they were in the colony): *Henceforth and forevermore, young ladies may learn things necessary for the establishment of the well-being of the colony—government, law, architecture, mathematics, and science.*

Alas, soon Mr. Sewell, my disagreeable tutor, will arrive to instruct me in the *Book of Common Prayer,* and then Mother has more needlework for me to do. Brother John, however, tutored in many subjects I can only hope to read about one day, now goes to school most of the day. And then he shall have the finest education at Oxford University. I know Papa made sure I learned to read and write, and for that, I am truly grateful. If only Papa would let the tutor teach me what John studies. Why give me the key to this incredible world of learning but lock me away from everything it could open?

Dear friend, I already miss you so much! You were the only one who really understood this heart's desire and who did not mock me for it. Your heart for adventure is taking you far, far away from me and I cannot bear it. If only I was on that ship with you.

Your friend,

Elizabeth

Somewhere
in the Atlantic Ocean

July 25, 1609

Dear Elizabeth,

This note must be short, and I do not know if you will ever have an opportunity to read it. But even if I drown, there is still a chance that this note could reach you. I want you to know that you have been my dearest friend ever, and I love you.

We are experiencing terrible gales and winds. The ship lists from side to side, and we are deathly afraid it will blow over. All hands are on deck—even Father—and he is not a sailor. I heard someone say it is a hurricane. If it is, we may all be doomed. Oh dearest Elizabeth, have I left my home and friends only to die on the way to my adventure? I must go. We are all needed to bail water.

Your friend forever,
even in heaven,

Abigail

Chipping Camden, England

JULY 12, 1609

Dear Abigail,

It has been exactly one month since you left, and I long for a letter from you. Papa has heard nothing either. Surely as one of the stockholders of the Virginia Company that sponsored your fleet, he would be among the first to learn of your arrival. I miss you so much. This waiting to learn of your safe passage is unbearable.

Papa sent me to the country to stay with my aunt and uncle. Ever since the fever that killed so many children in London four years ago, Papa whisks me out of the city and into the country air as much as possible during the summer. I do not mind though. Uncle has an exquisite library, and he has told me I may read anything here I desire. I only wish Papa felt the same way. They may be brothers, but their ideas of education are worlds apart.

I escape for long walks in the woods until I find just the right spot to spend an entire afternoon reading. I am fond of books about nature at present.

Write soon, dear friend! I miss you so.

Devotedly,

Elizabeth

Chipping Camden, England

Dear Abigail,

Still no word! I received a letter from Papa yesterday with great hopes that one from you would be tucked inside. But nothing! Papa said there is still no word about the fate of the ship on which you sailed. He does not say much, but I can tell he is worried too. I suppose it is too soon for letters to arrive from Virginia, but we were hoping for some word from a passing ship that arrived in London.

Today my aunt and I traveled by coach to the market. We spent a goodly part of the day overseeing the sale of our wool, spun into the softest yarn in the country. My job was to collect the coins and make the change. I was glad my aunt trusted me to do the proper figures and to keep the books for our sales. In the late afternoon, just before the close of the market, we purchased soap, cinnamon, writing paper, ink, wax candles, and some silk stockings for my aunt from a traveling merchant.

I know I prattle on about my comings and goings in my letters. It is a simple life here, but one where my education is valued. My aunt does not say it in so many words, but I do believe she thinks it is important to learn. Tonight I found a copy of a new book she left by my bedside: *A Booke of Divers Medecines* by Mrs. Corylon. Perhaps she saw my collection of medicinal herbs in the basket in the window. I could never be a physician or even an apothecary, as that is for men, but I do love to learn how to make remedies.

Your friend,

Elizabeth

On Solid Ground in the Colony of Virginia

AUGUST 18, 1609

Dearest Elizabeth,

I must write this posthaste even though it will be weeks, perhaps months before you receive this letter. Mother and Father and I are well—but many have been lost.

Several weeks into our journey, the sky darkened to a deep black. The wind tossed the *Blessing* to and fro for three days. Our ship lost contact with all the others. The blackness of the night continued even into day as waves as high as the sky washed over the deck.

As the hull filled with water, women and children below took buckets, scooped water from the body of the ship and handed them to the next person in line. At the end of the line below the deck, one of the men lifted them up to the other men on the deck, who threw the water overboard. Our courageous captain instructed all of us in what to do. He never appeared frightened. But I was terrified.

Finally, the winds calmed down. We had not slept for three days, and we were all surprised that the *Blessing* was still afloat. We cheered our captain who, though weary, was much relieved. The captain recharted our course. It seems that Admiral Somers had instructed the captains to head to Bermuda if the ships became separated.

A week after the winds calmed, the *Blessing* caught up with the *Lion* and the *Falcon*. I was ever so glad to see Temperance Flowerdew on the deck of the *Falcon*. The *Unity* was sore distressed—only the captain and one poor sailor were left alive. As the winds were strong for Virginia, the captains of the ships decided to head that way. We landed just one week ago. Yesterday, the *Diamond* and then the *Sparrow* docked. The *Sparrow* was barely afloat. The only ships left to arrive are the *Sea Venture* and one small supply vessel. There was great joy when we all were on the ground again, but our rejoicing was short-lived.

The wonderful new home we were all looking forward to is in great distress. Many of the people in the colony are sick. The colony is ill-prepared for so many new arrivals. There is precious little food or shelter. The bugs are horrible. I swat at my face and arms most of the day. It is hot and miserable.

Father speaks in hushed tones with Mother about the Indians as well. I know they are as fearful as I am. We heard that some of the Indians trade with the English, but there have been many more reports of the savagery of some of the tribes. No English girls have been here before. Will they leave us alone or kidnap us? Father says I must always stay inside the fort. He must be worried too.

Last night I heard the snap of a branch underfoot. I held my breath. Did I imagine it? Was it a deer? Or were they out there—at the palisade fence walls of the fort? Watching? Waiting? Please pray for us!

Your friend,

Abigail

Chipping Camden, England

AUGUST 22, 1609

Dear Abigail,

Tomorrow I leave for London. Uncle slipped me a present wrapped in paper and tied with a string. He says I am not to open it until I return to London. I have felt around the edges. It is a book! I wonder which one it is?

Oh, my dear, dear uncle. He probably knows it is the last book of any interest that I shall be allowed to read for a while. Soon Master Sewell will come calling to instruct me in the Christian faith and music, but nothing more. My mind simply must have more to fill it.

I am eager to learn everything I can about this world. Papa told me John will study astronomy this year in school. I too want to learn about the heavens and the stars. Why is it only something a boy can learn? I am good at figures. I could calculate the paths of stars. If only Papa would let me.

Tonight, however, I did not study the stars—I danced under them. Our coach arrived at Heathcoate Manor at six o'clock. I wore a violet damask gown trimmed with lace. You remember it? It is the one Mother bought for me at the Royal Exchange this spring. My aunt lent me a necklace of amethysts and pearls that glistened in the moonlight against my dress. She helped comb my hair and my ordinarily unruly curls looked beautiful as they spilled down on my neck.

Apparently, some of the young gentlemen thought I looked agreeable as well for I danced nearly every dance! I wish you had been there. It would have made it all so much more wonderful to have shared this evening with you.

Tomorrow I journey home to London—and hopefully, to news about you.

Your friend,

Elizabeth

James Towne, Virginia

AUGUST 26, 1609

Dear Elizabeth,

We are hungry. The food we had on the ships spoiled from the seawater getting into it. We have no place to sleep but under the stars. Many are sick. The new leaders of the colony, with orders from the king to govern the colony, are on the *Sea Venture*, and it has not yet arrived. There is much bickering among the leaders about who will govern if the *Sea Venture* has been lost. No wonder the king wanted to replace these leaders with new ones.

With each week that passes, we grow more anxious about the *Sea Venture*. I overheard Mother trying to comfort Mistress Pierce. She fears her husband, who traveled with the other leaders on it, is lost. What would it be like for little Jane to lose her father so young? I could not imagine life without Father, not in this fearful place.

Captain John Smith is furious with other so-called leaders, especially Captain Ratcliffe. He took men to Point Comfort to build a stockade. Others have been sent out to look for food.

I must close now. I hope you have heard word of the *Sea Venture* and that they are safe as well. Little Jane cries herself to sleep each night with worry about her father.

Your friend,

Abigail

London, England

Dearest Abigail,

I have been worried sick. Oh, how I hate to wait for news. I pray you made it there safely and that I will hear from you before too long. Mother tells me I should think good thoughts of you and not the worst, and so I will.

I imagine the colonists there were quite happy to see all the ships arrive. What did they think of the horses? Where are you living? Did you find a wonderful home waiting for you? Please give my love to your dear parents, and know that I am thinking of you now in August, no matter when you actually receive this letter.

Master Sewell arrives tomorrow, and my dreaded tutoring begins again. Mother greeted me upon my return from Uncle's home, asked all about my time in Chipping Camden, and then promptly put some new needlework in my hands. I wish it were a book she put in my hands instead.

That reminded me of Uncle's present. Tonight after I bade my parents good night, I opened his present. Yes, it was a book, but I was quite surprised at what he had sent to me. It is a New Testament—in Greek! I knew instantly why he had chosen it.

Tomorrow I shall approach Papa with utmost decorum and in my most persuasive manner seek his leave to study the Greek language with Master Sewell. Oh, how can Papa object to such a singular request of one eager to learn more of her faith in its original language? Uncle is so dear and so clever!

Your devoted friend,

Elizabeth

James Towne, Virginia

AUGUST 31, 1609

Dear Elizabeth,

We are under much pressure now. Our two blacksmiths work night and day making nails for the new homes. The newcomers must build as many homes as possible inside the fort before winter. We will likely have several families in each home.

I hope we are with Captain and Mistress Pierce and little Jane. I am quite fond of them. Captain Tucker told Mistress Pierce that if anyone can survive a hurricane, it is Captain Pierce. Yet, we still have had no word about the *Sea Venture.*

For now, we are in a lean-to made of small trees and mats woven of reeds from the marsh. My fingers are cut all over from the effort. Mother and I soak the reeds in water until they are soft and then weave them back and forth until we have a strong, tight mat.

Father says our work will keep the rain from soaking us, and he keeps us in good spirits as we weave. Temperance is not at all interested in weaving mats. I do not think she was ready for this adventure at all.

Your friend,

Abigail

Liberty Letters

Escape on the Underground Railroad

kidz

Nancy LeSourd

Philadelphia, Pennsylvania

FOURTH MONTH 27, 1858

Dear Hannah,

I've done it again. This is the third time in as many months that I've brought it up. It was no sooner out of my mouth than I wished I could take it back.

I graduate from Friends Central High in two years, and if I am going to enter Female Medical College, I need to study physiology now. There is so much to learn. And what I really need is a skeleton. So, I asked my parents. Again. For the third time. Big mistake.

Father rambled on about a proper Quaker woman's aspirations. You know, husband, children, home, and service. I reminded him that the Medical College was started by Quakers for Quaker women, and that I could serve by healing others, but he pretended he didn't hear me.

Mother put down her stitching and simply said, "There will be no dead bones in this home."

I promised her Friend Bones (as I like to call him just as I would any other beloved Quaker friend) would be very well behaved. "Friend Bones won't rattle around because I'll hang him from a pole in my room so I can study him better."

Mother tilted her head and began to answer. She stopped short and studied me. It was almost as if she were going to relent, but then, me and my big mouth, I had to fill the silence, didn't I? "Friend Bones," I blurted out, "will be quite at home here. Like one of the family." Mother got up, said she had washing to do, and that was that.

Sometimes I think Father regrets bringing me home from Springdale Boarding School right next door to you and enrolling me at Friends Central High, here in the city. Although Father definitely believes in the equality of all men, regardless of race, I'm not sure he agrees that applies to equality of all men *and women.* Father is not comfortable with the idea of a woman being a doctor.

At the rate I am going, however, it will be a long time before I can become a doctor. Friends Central doesn't offer more-advanced science courses. I guess I shouldn't complain though. Even the boys can't take physiology.

When I'm not pestering my parents about Friend Bones, we spend more and more time working together on getting delivery packages safely to their destinations. Yet, it's more dangerous now than ever to be in the delivery business. And complicated. There are many who would see us fail. The stakes are much higher now — with grave penalties. Ask your grandfather to explain. I should close for now.

Your friend,

Sarah

Goose Creek, Virginia

SIXTH MONTH 2, 1858

Dear Sarah,

I helped Grandfather survey another road today. His map of Loudoun County has been well received and he wants to get this next map published soon. I hope so, because he might take me with him to visit his publisher in Philadelphia ... and you!

Joshua came along again to help. He's seventeen and is Uncle Richard's apprentice at the foundry. Although he is only a year older than I am, our lives are so different. He's been an orphan for twelve years now, and ever since, he has had to work to earn his food and lodging.

As usual, I kept the notebook and carefully wrote down everything Grandfather called out to me as he and Joshua worked the chain and compass to measure the road. Joshua and Grandfather can make calculations in their heads faster than I can write them down.

I waited for my chance. When Joshua started to roll up the surveying chain, I showed Grandfather your letter. He read it quickly, then glanced at Joshua, and whispered that I was not to say a word about this to anyone. On the way home, Joshua tried to make me laugh, but my mind was too preoccupied with questions. What is this delivery business that you're involved in? Why is Grandfather being so mysterious? Why won't he talk about it with Joshua around?

After supper, Grandfather asked me to come to the barn with him to brush down Frank. You remember Frank, don't you? Such a solid horse, deserving of such a solid name. Grandfather brushed away some of the hay in Frank's stall and showed me a trapdoor.

Grandfather did not say a word. He just let me look inside with my lamp. I saw a bed of straw and a blanket. I stared inside for a long time. Then Grandfather lowered the trapdoor and spread the hay over it again. Frank nuzzled me, but I could not move. I shivered in the night air even though it was quite warm. Thoughts, questions whirled around in my head.

Grandfather put his hands on my shoulders and said, "The Lord said he came to proclaim liberty to the captives — to set free those in bondage. How can we do any less?" He glanced over his shoulder and continued, "It is fourteen miles from our home to the Potomac River. Once a slave crosses that river, it is but a short journey through Maryland to Pennsylvania … and freedom."

We walked back to the house in silence. Then I lit my candle stub and came straight to my room to write this letter. I know many of our faith are part of what they call the Underground Railroad, but Grandfather? Sarah, is your family part of this Underground Railroad too? Are these the packages you spoke about? Why are you in danger? Don't you live in a free state? How long has Grandfather been hiding slaves right here at Evergreen? Are we in danger too? I have so many questions. I cannot sleep.

Your friend,
Hannah

Philadelphia, Pennsylvania

SIXTH MONTH 14, 1858

Dear Hannah,

I shared your letter with Mother. She says we must not speak of such things by letter, especially by any letter posted in Virginia. She has a plan, though. Your grandfather arrives tomorrow. I'll send a special present back with him for you.

I have worked my fingers to the bone sewing all week. We need shirts, lots of shirts. I'll explain more later. Hannah, I'm afraid that our friendship quilt must wait a bit longer. There is not time right now to work on it.

I had a brilliant idea to win Father over about Friend Bones. I think he's worried I want to live in a man's world and am not dedicated to becoming a proper Quaker woman. So, today I rode the horse-drawn omnibus to Forty-Fourth and Haverford to volunteer at the Association for the Care of Colored Orphans. Right now there are 67 boys and girls, from babies to nine year olds, living at the Shelter.

I asked the director if I could help with nursing the children when they are sick. Sounds noble, but I figured that with this many children here, the doctor is likely to stop by often. So, maybe I could learn medicine while I help out. Mrs. Whitaker said right now she needs my help to tutor the older children in reading, writing, and basic computations.

Mrs. Whitaker told me about a new boy who arrived last week. He's seven years old, and his name is Zebulon Coleman. I glanced in his direction. "He seems scared," I commented.

Mrs. Whitaker nodded. "The children are often frightened when they first arrive. New surroundings. New people." She lowered her voice to a whisper. "Something terrible happened to Zebulon's parents, so he may need more time to adjust."

I started to ask her what happened, but she turned and walked over to Zebulon to introduce him to me.

Zebulon didn't speak when I greeted him. He lowered his eyes and stared at the same spot on the floor. I tried my best to let him know I was friendly, but his eyes didn't budge.

I wonder what happened to Zebulon's family.

On the way out, I bumped into a man with a suitcase. He tipped his hat and said, "Peter Pennington, at your service."

I said hello but felt uneasy.

He continued, "New girl, eh? Going to help out?"

I brushed past him without an answer. How did he know who I was? What business is it of his anyway? Who is this man? I hope he isn't staying here.

Your friend,

Sarah

Goose Creek, Virginia

SIXTH MONTH 25, 1858

Dear Sarah,

As soon as Grandfather arrived home, I asked about my present from you. He smiled and handed me a little seedling in a big clay pot. Not exactly what I was expecting from my best friend. You know I can get tree seedlings from Grandfather's nursery any time I want.

After a few moments he said, "Hannah, thee is so disappointed! Come with me. There is more to this little seedling than meets the eye."

Grandfather led me to a table in the greenhouse and turned the pot upside down. All the dirt not attached to the roots rolled out onto the table, as did a small leather pouch. Inside were your letters!

What a magnificent idea your mother had to hide your letters in a pot. Now when I write back, Grandfather will carry my letters to you the same way. It's just another pot with other cuttings from our nursery here at Evergreen to sell in Philadelphia. No one will ever guess our secret. If we must speak about things better left unspoken, this will do quite nicely.

Grandfather had another surprise for me. A buyer for the cuttings from the Ginko tree did not have enough cash to make the purchase. Instead, he opened a velvet pouch of pearls and other gems. Grandfather selected a perfect, milky white pearl in payment. He said that when he saw it, he thought of me and wanted me to have this as a token of his love for me.

Have you worked on our friendship quilt lately? I will take my leather pouch to bed tonight and read your letters by candlelight.

Your friend,
Hannah

Philadelphia, Pennsylvania

Sixth Month 28, 1858

Dear Hannah,

By now you have my letters in hand. Were you surprised? It's a lot to think about, I know. There's more you need to know.

One night while your grandfather was here, Mr. Robert Purvis from the Anti-Slavery Vigilance Committee came to speak with Father about a package that was delivered here for our care—a slave from Maryland who escaped two weeks ago. Mother and I sat quietly, mending shirts for the fugitives, and listened intently to the men as they talked.

Ever since the passage of the Fugitive Slave Act, fugitive slaves who live in free states can be recaptured and sent back to slavery. The Committee works harder than ever now to get the escaped slaves all the way to Canada.

The slave catchers pay for information to identify a fugitive slave who is now working in the city. The Committee has to be even more careful in order to keep a runaway here in the city. Names must be changed, and sometimes even that isn't enough. Now, more than ever, you've got to know who can be trusted.

Your grandfather said it's harder than ever to help slaves to freedom in Virginia too. As the largest slave state in the country, the Virginia plantation owners are known to help slave owners from other states find their "property" that has escaped north.

He told us that for several months now the slave catchers and their hounds come by Evergreen routinely. He suspects that it is more an attempt to scare him, but your grandfather does not frighten easily. He told us that sheriffs in Culpeper tell these slave catchers it is well known that if a slave makes it to Evergreen, he will make it to freedom. Father and Mr. Purvis laughed because, well, it is true!

Mr. Purvis encouraged your grandfather to step up his efforts, because now more than ever, the Railroad must operate quickly. The demand is great and experienced conductors who can be trusted are valuable to the movement. Mr. Purvis said he firmly believes that the skill your grandfather has in mapmaking was given to him by God to assist those in bondage.

Father said your grandfather knows every road, path, canal, and creek in Loudoun County, and if anyone can help slaves in their run to freedom, it is Friend Yardley Taylor.

Your grandfather may need your help. After Mr. Purvis left, your grandfather said his hearing is not what it used to be. He said he needs to be nimble to help the slaves but that carting around his heavy, awkward ear trumpet to be able to hear slows him down.

Now that he has shown you the hiding place, you have a special responsibility to ask God what he would have you do with this knowledge. When your grandfather showed you the straw bed, did you not think of the comfort of your own bed with its pillow? When your grandfather showed you the blanket just big enough to cover the straw bed, did you not think of your own ample covers and warm fire inside? Can you turn away from those God brings to your door at Evergreen? Hannah, I hope I have not offended you. But you have a good heart and you must think about what I have said.

I took the omnibus to the Shelter this afternoon. Mrs. Whitaker told me she wants me to work mostly with Zebulon. He was part of a small group of slaves who escaped from Alabama. The Committee split up the ones who made it this far to send them on to Canada by way of various delivery stations. Zebulon will stay here, at least until he is nine. Then they will find work for him so he can learn a skill and have a place to live until he is eighteen.

I asked Mrs. Whitaker what happened to Zebulon's parents, but she only said, "It's a very difficult story — one I will tell you when the time is right. Just know this. Zebulon needs to know you can be a true friend to him."

I don't know how I can show him I am his friend if he won't even talk to me. I tried to get Zebulon to respond to me, but he won't even look at me. He shied away from me when I came close.

I pulled up a chair and sat as close to him as he would allow, and began to read a story out loud with as much expression and enthusiasm as I could. About halfway through the story, I saw him look up at me out of the corner of his eye. When I met his gaze, however, he went right back to staring at the floor.

I kept my eyes on the pages of the book. When I sensed he was looking at me again, I shifted my position so that Zebulon could see the pictures in the book while I read the story. I didn't dare look directly at him. He leaned in a bit. Too soon the story was finished and Zebulon scurried away without a sound.

Oh Hannah, there is just something about that little boy. I must reach him.

On the way out, I almost ran into Peter Pennington. "Good day," he said. He whisked past me and called out for Mrs. Whitaker. I decided to stay and find out what he wanted. I hung back and watched him open his suitcase and begin to pull out lots of different objects. Bars of soap, candles of various sizes, sealing wax, envelopes, writing paper, socks, knitting needles, yarn, sewing thread and needles. So, he's a peddler. Still, the man gives me the creeps. I don't like him.

Your friend,

Sarah

Goose Creek, Virginia

SEVENTH MONTH 1, 1858

Dear Sarah,

What are you talking about? Slave patrols? At Evergreen? I haven't seen any slave patrols. Perhaps I don't want to. I know I've heard dogs at night, but I never thought they could be slave patrols. You've told me more about Grandfather's railroad business than he has. But I really don't want to know about it at all—from you or Grandfather.

I like my life the way it is. Simple. Predictable. Safe! Nothing but chores and cooking, school and surveying. You'll see. Wait until I tell you about my day. It's a simple life. There's no danger and no excitement—except for the hogs.

Our fire had gone out overnight. Mother sent me to Springdale Boarding School for some fire early this morning after I finished milking the cows.

Then I churned the butter. I have never minded milking the cows, but the steady pounding and repetition of making butter in the churn is so tiresome. What the cow gives in minutes takes hours of churning. Best to just drink the milk, I say.

We had a lot of baking to do for the picnic this week. We made seven pies out of the dewberries, gooseberries, and peaches I picked yesterday.

This afternoon, I gathered an armload of corn from the corncrib and began to call for the hogs. "P-o-o-o-e. P-o-o-o-e. P-o-o-o-e." The hogs were rooting around in the leaves on the ground for food, but when they heard me, they poked their noses up in the air, sniffed, and then came tearing down the hill. Their snorting and squealing filled the air. Three of them galloped down the hill so fast, they began to bump against each other.

I laughed so hard that I didn't jump out of the way soon enough, and the hogs knocked me down. The corn flew up in the air and

Liberty Letters

Secrets of Civil War Spies

 kidz

Nancy LeSourd

Richmond, Virginia

JUNE 17, 1861

Dear Emma,

I couldn't believe my eyes. "Private Franklin Thompson, of the Second Michigan Volunteers," you said. "Requesting donations for the Union Army, ma'am."

While Great Auntie Belle scurried around, loading my arms with linens, food, and medicines, so many questions swirled around in my head. How did you get to Michigan? And what, pray tell, possessed you to enlist in the Union Army? As you carried the supplies outside to the ambulance, I barely heard you whisper, "You'll keep my secret, won't you?"

"Such a nice young man, Mollie," Great Auntie commented, arms filled with more donations.

Young man? This is no man—this is Emma! I thought. *Emma, my good friend.* Last summer I was shocked when you confided in me that you left Canada with your mother's blessing to escape your cruel father. You even fooled everyone in New England, selling books disguised as a boy—one of Mr. Hurlburt's finest door-to-door salesmen. But this? A soldier in the war? Really, Emma! You've gone too far!

Your friend,

Mollie

Washington, D.C.

JUNE 22, 1861

Dear Mollie,

I know I need to explain. When Mr. Hurlburt offered me the chance to work in Flint, Michigan, I jumped at the chance to see more of this adopted country of mine. Mollie, I had to keep up my disguise. After all, I had to make a living.

Then I heard the newsboy cry out, "Fall of Fort Sumter — President's Proclamation — Call for 75,000 men!" It's true I'm not an American. When President Lincoln called for men to fight for my adopted country, I couldn't turn away. I had to help free the slaves. After much prayer, I knew God meant for me to enlist in the Army. So when my friends volunteered for the Second Regiment of the Michigan Volunteer Infantry, I assumed God would make a way for me too. But I missed the height requirement by two inches.

The day my friends left, the people of Flint cheered them on. The boys lined up with their bright bayonets flashing in the morning sunlight. Almost every family had a father, husband, son, or brother in that band of soldiers. The pastor preached a sermon and presented a New Testament to each one. Then as the bands played the "Star-Spangled Banner," the soldiers marched off to Washington. Oh, how I wanted to be with them!

A few weeks later, who should return to Flint, but my old friend from church, William Morse, now *Captain* William Morse who came back to recruit more soldiers for his regiment. This time I was ready. I stuffed my shoes with paper and stood as tall as I could. It worked! I was now Private Franklin Thompson of Company F of the Second Michigan Volunteer Infantry of the United States Army.

When I got to Washington, the army assigned me to be a field nurse. All the field nurses are men, and it doesn't matter if you don't have any training as a nurse. They tell us we'll learn it all from the field surgeons as we go. I reported to the Surgeon in charge and received my first order to visit the temporary hospitals set up all over the city. Although there are no battle injuries yet, many are sick with typhoid and malaria. There are not enough beds for the sick; not enough doctors to treat them; and not enough medicines and food.

That's why some of us decided to visit the good ladies of Washington and plead with them to donate to the Union. That was the day I saw you again—a most fortunate day for me. I hope you feel the same.

Your friend,

Private Frank Thompson, Company F,

Second Michigan Regiment

(Emma)

Richmond, Virginia

Dear Emma,

Of course, I was glad to see you again, but just how do you think you can pull this off—being a private in the United States Army? Sure you can handle nursing duties. But what about shooting and riding a horse, marching and drilling, standing guard and picket duty? Can you keep your secret much longer?

Great Auntie has arranged for our letters to get to each other through her private courier now that the federal government has suspended mail to the Southern states. She is delighted I want to write to a Federal soldier. I'll address your letters to Frank so there is no suspicion. Is it all right to call you Emma in the letter? I don't want to give you away.

Great Auntie makes no secret of her support of the North, as you saw from her willingness to part with supplies for the Union. To the great embarrassment of my Richmond kin, Great Uncle Chester is now a surgeon with the Union Army and Great Auntie Belle is an outspoken supporter of President Lincoln. If Daddy were still alive, I'm sure he would agree. At least that's what I think. Momma seems to think differently.

When Momma and I arrived at Mrs. Whitfield's home today to sew uniforms for the soldiers, we heard angry voices before we even entered the room. Mrs. Whitfield told the ladies she had personally delivered a handwritten invitation to Miss Elizabeth Van Lew and her mother to join us to sew for the Confederate soldiers, but the Van Lews refused to come.

"Let's not forget they sent their daughter, Betty, to that Quaker school in Philadelphia," an outraged Mrs. Morris reminded everyone. "They filled that child's head with abolition talk, and it changed her forever."

"That they did," Mrs. Forrest agreed. "And when Mr. Van Lew died, Betty talked her mother into freeing all their slaves."

Aunt Lydia added, "I heard they even sent one of their slave girls up north to Philadelphia for her schooling and paid for it all!"

I watched the ladies ram their needles through the flannel shirts they were stitching with as much force as the words they were speaking. Personally, I think these ladies are petty gossips. So what if Miss Van Lew believes what the Union does? Is that a crime? It seems so. If they only knew what I believed, they would not permit me in their company. A Southern girl with Northern thoughts. I kept my head down as these ladies spoke. I didn't want them to see the fire in my eyes.

I excused myself as soon as I could and slipped out without much notice. No one pays much attention to a sixteen-year-old girl these days. The women worry about their boys and men and speak endlessly of the impending battles. Their attention is not on the comings and goings of someone like me.

I took this package to the place the courier designated to drop off our letters. I may have knitted for the Confederates today, but this pair of socks is included for you, my adventurous Union friend. Perhaps they will keep your feet from blistering on those long marches.

Your friend,

Mollie

Washington, D.C.

JULY 1, 1861

Dear Mollie,

Thanks for thinking about how to protect my secret. To tell the truth, I like reading my name again. To these men, I am just Frank, but to you, my good friend, I am Emma. I keep your letters tucked inside my shirt so no one can read them. I suppose for now, though, you should continue to address your letters to Frank, but just call me E in the letter. If I should lose a letter, I don't want to risk being found out.

As for riding a horse or shooting a gun, what do you think I did all those years when I was growing up on our farm in New Brunswick, Canada? I can outride and outshoot most anyone—thank you, Miss Mollie. If God has called me to this, then he has prepared me and equipped me to do what I must do. Farming was no harder work. Just try chopping and clearing the land some time, Mollie. Why, you should have seen me swing my ax to hew beams from timber as fast as the next boy. No sirree, if I'm found out, it will not be because I failed to hold my own with these brave men.

Washington is overrun with soldiers. White tents dot the landscape all around the city. The Capitol and the White House shelter hundreds of soldiers, who sit around playing cards and wait for action. Thousands of soldiers drill in the streets. Blasts from bugles and the rat-tat-tat of drums fill the air. All are eager to fight. The rebellion should be put down quickly.

Your friend,

Emma

Richmond, Virginia

JULY 4, 1861

Dear Emma,

Richmond celebrated Independence Day today, but I had to wonder, is it independence from England years ago or independence from the North it celebrates? Sissy asked me to go with her today to the camps outside the city to watch the soldiers drill. She may be two years older than I, but she has such romantic notions about this war. She thinks she can send her Lemuel off to war and he will return to her a hero. Our friends ride out to the camps every day. They dress up, bring their picnic foods, and wait for the drills to end so they can socialize with the soldiers. It all seems so silly to me—this partying with soldiers. Soldiers and girls alike think we will simply wallop the North in one big battle, and then it'll all be over. I'm not so sure.

I don't agree with you that this will be a short war. You think the boys in blue will crush the boys in gray. But here in Richmond, we too have white tents dotting the landscape like snow. Our soldiers march day and night, eager to meet the enemy. We too have hundreds, if not thousands, of young men who are certain we will capture Washington and take over the White House and Capitol where your soldiers now lounge. I do not think victory will come so easily, my dear friend, not to either side.

As the South Carolina regiment marched past us, the girls waved their handkerchiefs and cheered. They debated which regiment is the most handsome. The general consensus of our friends is that the boys from South Carolina are definitely the best looking, although the Texas regiment is a close runner-up with their rugged good looks. You see how deep their thoughts go about this war, Emma. Skin deep.

My attention was on two women handing out food and flowers to the South Carolinians. A murmur spread through the crowd. It was Miss Van Lew and her mother who smiled as they handed out their gifts. Miss Van Lew called out, "May God grant victory to the righteous!" Very clever. She didn't say which side is righteous! But the boys seemed to enjoy her attentions just the same. The women who whispered behind their fans as they watched certainly were wondering why a supposed Yankee loyalist brings food to the Confederate soldiers!

Great Auntie wrote that I can't return to Mrs. Pegram's school next fall. For the past two years since Daddy died, the Greats (that's what I call them) have paid for my education. Mrs. Pegram, with three sons fighting for the South, returned their money, and told them that Federal dollars are worthless to purchase an education for a Confederate girl. She said they could exchange their money for Confederate scrip and resend the funds for my semester's tuition.

Of course, that made the Greats furious. As much as they value my education, they won't put it ahead of their beliefs. Great Auntie prepared a box of books from Great Uncle Chester's library and sent them to me to study on my own. It's not the same though. This war is turning everything upside down.

My good friend Charlie brought the newspapers tonight and tried to cheer me up. The Confederates captured the Union steamer, the *St. Nicholas*. The paper reported that Madame LaForce—an outrageously dressed, veiled lady—boarded at Baltimore with great fanfare and seven dress trunks. Madame LaForce flirted with the sailors in French and English, but you should have seen her later when she pulled pistols and swords, not dresses, out of those trunks. Madame LaForce was really Colonel Thomas! "She" created such a distraction that no one noticed the eight men who boarded the *St. Nicholas* at Port Comfort that day and then joined Colonel Thomas in the attack on the ship that night. Later, the *St. Nicholas* captured several other Union ships filled with supplies that can now go to the Confederate Army.

My good friend Emma posing as a Union soldier, and a Confederate colonel posing as a lady. All is definitely not what it first appears!

Your friend,

Mollie

Richmond, Virginia

July 7, 1861

Dear E,

I just got your most recent letter and will do as you suggest. I want to do all I can to help you keep this secret.

Yesterday Sissy married Lemuel Hastings. And today he enlisted in the Army of the Confederate States of America. Sissy is determined to follow him wherever he is sent to fight. Momma told Sissy that her place is in Richmond with the ladies, sewing uniforms, knitting socks, and rolling bandages. Sissy bounced out of the room with her skirts swishing behind her as she tossed her head full of blonde curls. "I shall follow Lemuel to the ends of the earth," she called back to us over her shoulder. "It is my wifely duty."

Sissy has always been impulsive, but she gave Momma only three days to pull together a wedding. Even with the help of Momma's kin and their servants, there was hardly enough time to decorate the parlor, bake and display the cakes and sweets, and deliver all the invitations. Sissy decided there should be no wedding gifts. Not that anyone has any money to spare right now, anyway. In her usual fashion, she turned that all to her advantage. In her noblest of voices, she announced to one and all that they should each bring a necessity for the Confederate soldiers and deposit it in the box by the front door.

I honestly don't believe that Sissy understands what this is all about. Ever since Daddy died, it's like Sissy refuses to grow up. She'd rather pretend nothing is wrong than face facts. That's how she is with Lem and this war. She probably thinks she will pull on her white kidskin gloves, button up her dainty shoes, and swirl her hooped skirt around her as she travels by train or coach to the nearest town where Lemuel's unit is stationed. Then when he is off duty, they will dance the night away at the local town hall.

Your friend,

Mollie

Richmond, Virginia

JULY 10, 1861

Dear E,

Sissy and I walked to Pizzini's for ice cream. With each bite, Sissy complained about the Union blockade of our ports. If it succeeds, we will be unable to get the necessities of life. To Sissy, this means her tea and sweets. She hoards sugar in a tin can in her room. She says she may have to suffer many things in this war, but she will not suffer the loss of her sugar.

Sissy says she wants this silly war to get started so those horrible Yanks can be put in their place and her dear Lem can come home to her. I suppose that's what you are to most of those I know here: a horrible Yank.

The Northern papers Great Auntie sent me urge you Federals to stop the "Rebel Congress" from meeting here next week. "Forward to Richmond! On to Richmond! The Rebel Congress shall not meet." I admit I'm frightened. Momma too. She speaks in hushed tones with the Richmond kin. They are especially quiet around Sissy. They don't want her to be frightened for Lemuel. But how can she not be frightened? Won't he be one of the ones defending our dear city?

Will you be the one attacking it? I do not like this at all.

Your friend,

Mollie

Richmond, Virginia

July 17, 1861

Dear E,

Just three days until the Confederate government meets here. People talk quietly, especially when there are children in the room. It's not like they don't notice. The adults pretend we're safe in our homes, but you can hear the sounds of the guns and drummers on the battlefields not that far away. Sissy sits at the window, twisting her handkerchief first one way then the other. Momma told her to knit to keep her fingers busy. Sissy tried, but gave up in frustration, dropping more stitches than she could keep on the needles.

I suggested a walk. Old men spoke in hushed tones in doorways. Women whispered to one another behind fans. Only the youngest children seemed carefree. Would the Union win and be "On to Richmond"? What about the dozens of fathers, husbands, brothers, and sons that enlisted? Would they return?

Tonight Momma and the Richmond ladies gathered at Aunt Lydia's home to roll bandages and pick lint for packing wounds. Momma asked Sissy and me to come with her. I wish we were knitting socks and sewing uniform shirts. I don't like preparing for wounds and cuts and bloody bodies. I shudder to think of it. Sissy tries to join in, but I can see on her face she is wondering if the bandage she rolls tonight will be on her husband tomorrow.

Your friend,

Mollie

Adventures in Jamestown
Softcover • ISBN 9780310713920

Londoner Abigail Matthews, a daring adventurer, moves to Jamestown
and then Henricus, Virginia, where she comes to know Pocahontas, who
was captured by the settlers. Her best friend Elizabeth Walton, still in
England, encourages Abigail to see past her hurt and anger to befriend
this most unlikely of companions. Excellent for educators and homeschool use.

Available now at your local bookstore!

Liberty Letters

Escape on the Underground Railroad
Softcover • ISBN 9780310713913

Together, two girls living a world apart must outwit slave catchers
and assist a runaway South Carolina slave girl on her perilous trip
from Virginia to Canada on the Underground Railroad. Excellent for
educators and homeschool use.

Available now at your local bookstore!

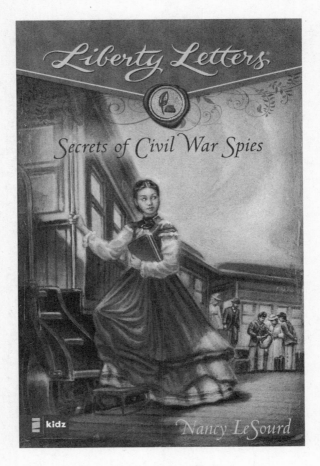

Secrets of Civil War Spies
Softcover • ISBN 9780310713906

As the United States is torn apart in the early days of the Civil War,
two girls risk everything for what they believe to preserve the Union.
Emma, a Yankee, finds creative ways to keep her identity secret, while
her southern friend Mollie must decide if she, too, will spy on the
Confederacy. Excellent for educators and homeschool use.

Available now at your local bookstore!

We want to hear from you. Please send your comments about this book to us in care of zreview@zondervan.com. Thank you.

ZONDERVAN.com/
AUTHORTRACKER
follow your favorite authors